SOLITAIRE

VOLUME 2
THE AGENDA

Airship 27 Productions

Solitaire (Volume 2)
The Agenda
© 2025 Lee Houston Jr.

Published by Airship 27 Productions
www.airship27.com
www.airship27hangar.com

Interior illustrations © 2025 Chuck Bordell
Cover illustration © 2025 Ted Hammond

Editor: Ron Fortier
Associate Editor: Gordon Dymowski
Marketing and Promotions Manager: Michael Vance
Production Designer: Rob Davis

ISBN: 978-1-969285-06-6

Produced in the United States of America

10 9 8 7 6 5 4 3 2 1

SOLITAIRE
VOLUME 2
THE AGENDA

BY
LEE HOUSTON, JUNIOR

DEDICATION
For my father, Lee Senior
October 25, 1936-April 19, 2024

CHAPTER 1

Despite its plushness, Ariel Andrews sat uncomfortably in the well padded chair. Her desk's large rectangular top was covered with folders full of business papers, which were occasionally referenced as she continued to intently work at her computer. Her neck and shoulder muscles were starting to ache, and she longed for rest. Yet except for brushing back a stray strand of blonde hair, she refused to quit until completing the task at hand, which was interrupted by a knock on her closed office door.

"Yes?" the busy executive said without bothering to look away from her monitor, for she knew who entered.

"Ma'am? It's after midnight. Is everything okay?" her personal assistant asked.

"Thanks for staying late Carol. I'm just making sure all the I's are dotted and the T's crossed so everything runs smoothly and we stay on top," Andrews replied, actually pausing to look at the older woman now standing before her.

"Part of the reason I'm still here too," Carol Evans reminded her, reaching out to attempt straightening the folders strewn across the desk.

"Leave those," her superior ordered, keeping the assistant from touching anything. "I'll take care of them before I call it a night."

"If you say so," Carol replied, privately noting some of the file tab labels while asking, "Do you need anything? Cup of coffee maybe?"

"Appreciate the offer, but I don't think I'll be here much longer," Andrews said, refusing to express the yawn building within. "Besides, we have to be back here by eight to prepare for that board meeting at ten. You go on home and I'll see you in the morning."

"If you insist. But you should too if you want to be sharp for—"

"I will be," Andrews promised, thinking about the fold out couch and the full private bath her office had, along with the spare changes of clothing she kept on the premises. "Night Carol."

"Good night," the assistant replied before reluctantly leaving the office.

When she was alone again, Ariel Andrews ignored the folders on her desk and pulled out those hidden within a drawer.

Ever since I took over Andrews Aviation with Dad's retirement, it's like

5

someone's been targeting the company, if not me specifically. An occasional shipping discrepancy I can understand. Regardless of their position, employees are human too. But practically every week? And all to a particular region? Whatever is going on, I intend to get to the bottom of it, she mused, comparing the printed pages to the computer screen readout.

+++

The worried lady was closer to the truth than she realized, for her trusted assistant had not gone very far. Carol looked around to confirm she was truly alone in the deserted corridor before making a discrete cellphone call.

"It's me," she began without preamble when the other party answered. "I don't think Andrews has actually discovered anything yet, but she is starting to wonder about things she shouldn't." Carol then reported the office encounter in full detail, finishing with "There's nothing crucial pending other than the upcoming prototype presentation. Yet I've never known her to stay this late over a regularly scheduled board meeting before."

"I see," the voice on the other end replied before pausing to think things over. "Continue as planned," it finally instructed. "Only act in case of emergency but remember, in the end she and the rest of the Andrews family are mine."

+++

Like any major city Miami, Florida had the attention getting bright lights of popular nighttime attractions, but also the hidden darkness behind the scenes that accompanied it.

As faint echoes of dance music could be heard from somewhere nearby, the luxury sedan pulled into the alley and stopped upon the cheaper tarred surface after its rear bumper cleared the concrete sidewalk.

The chauffeur stared straight ahead into the unknown but couldn't see beyond the high beams' edge, for the vehicle's headlights failed to pierce the Stygian darkness. "It is 12:37, so we are adhering to their schedule," he announced in a crisp British accent, after comparing the dashboard clock with his wristwatch. "But sir, are you sure about this?" he asked without turning to face his lone passenger.

"No, but if this is the only way to get Fredrick back..." the man in the rear of the car replied, leaving the rest unsaid.

"Understood, sir," the driver answered, before dimming the headlights to their normal setting and inching the automobile forward.

Traveling at such a slow crawl, those inside swore to hearing the tires roll across and crunch upon every individual piece of tarred gravel on their clandestine route.

While the only vehicle present since the many businesses that used that alley were closed for the night, there were times when the sedan barely managed to squeeze past trash dumpsters and other obstacles left askew. Each inch forward seemed like a mile in an endless quest with no hope of reaching either the end or at least a satisfactory conclusion to their mission.

The journey continued until about halfway through the man-made corridor, when an automobile parked somewhere in the darkness ahead of them suddenly turned on its high beam lights.

The driver stopped the sedan and raised one hand to shield his vision as armed gunmen emerged from the shadows that seemed to comprise most of the alley.

Having heard a tapping sound on his window, the chauffeur turned and saw the barrel of a handgun pointed directly at him.

"Yo, Jeeves. Turn off your lights and the engine, lower the window and hand me the keys," the gunman ordered. One hand held the weapon while the other was presented with palm open, awaiting the chauffeur's response.

"Sir?" The driver was actually talking to the passenger, but never took his eyes off the gun before him.

"Do as he says," replied the other man, looking through the closed rear window at the weapon pointed at him.

There were only two of them. Technically even odds but either man could shoot and kill before those inside the car had a chance to react.

"You shall have to wait a moment, for I cannot lower the window without the key being at least within the Accessories position," the chauffeur replied, but otherwise fully cooperated.

With everything done, the gunman took the keys from the driver and tossed them onto the automobile's roof.

As if on cue, the other car's headlights dimmed to their normal setting but still provided the assailants light to see by.

"Hands on the steering wheel Jeeves," the driver's side thug then ordered.

"It's actually Edgar, sir," the chauffeur replied in his proper English manner, unable to tear his eyes away from the killing end of the weapon still pointed at him.

"If you don't do what I say it's gonna be dead!"

"Y-yes, s-sir," Edgar stammered, complying with the request.

With that the man used his free hand to pull out a pair of handcuffs from a back pocket of his blue jeans while keeping the gun aimed. Soon Edgar found himself restrained to it in such a way that the steering wheel kept him from being able to use either hand, let alone free an arm.

"Now you, out of the car!" the other hoodlum ordered the passenger.

"Yes, sir," the man said meekly as he opened the door.

The chauffeur turned his head to the right the best he could and said, "Mister Andrews?"

"Don't worry Edgar. I'll be alright," he replied.

The passenger side hoodlum watched with a smile and tried to keep from laughing as Andrews attempted to comply. The balding but clean shaven, late middle-aged man's girth was more than first assumed, for he struggled to squeeze out the door because the sedan was parked too close to a building.

The criminal then had to take a step back as the now freed man fought to close the passenger door, which was scraping against the building wall.

As Andrews finally accomplished this task, the gunman ordered him up against the car with arms raised. The older man complied, while tightly holding the object of everyone's desire in his left hand.

Never once lowering his weapon, the thug frisked Andrews one handed. Excess flesh packed tightly within an expensive leisure suit gave here and there, but the final analysis was, "He's clean."

"Good," the man on the driver's side replied before briefly turning to address Edgar again. "Now stay quiet and you might actually live through this," he said with a smile before walking away.

The worried father asked, "Where's my son?"

The only response was the man beside him motioning straight past the car with his gun; to indicate in what direction their prisoner should start walking.

Finished with the driver, the first goon had moved to the front bumper and watched as their mark tried to squeeze his way between car and building to come forward. Yet neither gunman made a move to help.

Of more importance was the metal briefcase Andrews held onto tightly with his left hand. That they kept a close eye on without being too obvious as its bearer finally managed to clear the sedan's front bumper.

Andrews wanted to stop and catch his breath only to have the man behind him, who had no trouble at all traversing such a narrow space, order him to keep moving.

While it was only a scant few feet in length, as the briefcase bearer entered a makeshift clearing between the two vehicles, the car ahead suddenly put its brighter lights on again.

Temporarily blinded, Andrews raised his free hand to shield his eyes, the left with the case stayed by his side.

Then a shadow crossed in front of the alley's only light source as a male voice asked, "Reginald Andrews?"

"Yes. I presume you're Mister Jones," the worried father addressed the silhouette. It appeared to be of average height and build, but the headlights created shadows that prevented him from seeing more.

"For lack of a better alias. You have what I asked for?"

"Yes," Andrews meekly replied while holding up the briefcase for all to see. "Where's my son?"

"Business first," Jones said as he snapped his fingers.

Although there was no car door sounds to herald the action, someone came running up from the driver's side in response to the gesture.

While it was still fairly dark in the alley even with the other vehicle's headlights on, Reginald Andrews could make out that the man was in jeans and a plain T-shirt with a local soccer team's cap pulled down over his head to further obscure his facial features.

Andrews stood still as the man briefly waved an electronic device over him before concentrating on the briefcase.

A moment later the man stopped and ran back to Mister Jones. "All clear. No bugs or trackers," he announced, before disappearing to wherever he came from.

"Good," Jones replied before he snapped his fingers again.

This time there was the sound of a car door opening and closing before another man came forward from the shadows on the passenger side. He was escorting someone who had a hood over their head and arms behind their back.

The new arrivals stood to Jones' right in front of the car, with the hostage in the middle and somewhat blocking what light the vehicle provided.

"How do I know that's Fredrick?" Andrews asked, staring at the tall, skinny man standing between his captors.

Jones snapped his fingers again and the escort removed the hood.

Andrews and the unmasked man stared at each other.

It was hard for the older man to distinguish anyone's details in the harsh light, let alone the hostage's facial features.

Yet before the father could speak, the other man raised both arms.

That they were actually unbound was a minor revelation. But what they held was another matter as Reginald Andrews was shot twice in the chest with a 9mm handgun!

CHAPTER 2

Reginald Andrew's eyes widened in shock. Whether from the trauma of being shot or the possible identity of his assailant was a moot point as he clutched his chest with both hands, dropping the ransom filled briefcase. It hit the hard alley tarmac seconds before he did.

"I know my enemy and that wasn't Andrews! The real one is overweight but has a thick mustache!" the shooter yelled as he bent down to collect his spent bullet casings. "Grab the money and let's get out of here!"

"What about the chauffeur?" one of the men asked as the others rushed to comply.

The false hostage turned to stare at the sedan before saying, "He isn't worth the bullet. Let's go."

The alley echo of the last car door shutting was replaced by the squeal of tires rapidly going into motion as the other vehicle hastily backed away from the scene of the crime.

Having been in the Andrews family employ for decades, Edgar Wellington was shocked at what he witnessed. Tears were starting to leak from sad eyes, but it was with a clear and steady voice that the chauffeur said, "Emergency! Activate Aide Link!" knowing that despite the engine being off, the artificial intelligence of the sedan's internal systems would access energy from the car battery in automatic response to that key phrase.

"This is Aide Link. How can I help you?" a female voice replied.

"Call Police. Emergency!" he demanded, as the distant headlights shrank further to become two white dots.

Even as Edgar explained the situation and received a promise that help was being sent, he saw there must have been some point in the alley where the fleeing car was able to make a U-Turn. The white lights disappeared for a moment, then were replaced by two red pinpoints representing tail lights, which now totally faded from sight.

+++

The body laid perfectly still until long after any noise the escaping vehicle made faded into nonexistence.

Then the mysterious Samaritan some only knew as Solitaire rose to a sitting position.

Weighing far less than the real Reginald Andrews, the reddish contents of the pierced gel packs that comprised the special body suit's extra padding had drained through the bullet holes, staining the outer wear. The points of impact were still a tad sore, but the bulletproof vest underneath had kept bare flesh from actually being struck.

Besides being unarmed and unable to take the offensive because I had to stay in character, once they realized I had a vest on, one head shot would have permanently taken me out of the game, realized Solitaire, standing up. *Next move's mine, especially considering—*

Then the Clandestine Crusader noticed a shocked chauffeur staring at an alleged dead man.

Confidently, Solitaire walked over and in a different male voice said, "Don't panic. I'm just a disguised FBI agent wearing a bulletproof vest. Are you okay?"

All Edgar Wellington could do was just stare at the figure before him and nod affirmatively.

"Your employer is an important government contractor and among the top one hundred richest people at least on the Eastern seaboard, if not the continental United States. So, we certainly couldn't risk him making the ransom drop himself," Solitaire added, before hearing the faint notes of sirens in the distance growing louder. "Your doing?"

"Y-yes," Edgar replied, finally finding his voice. "Aide Link…"

"I understand. When they get here, tell the cops everything. Especially that that *wasn't* the real Fredrick Andrews with the kidnappers. There were six men, counting the driver. Based on what I was able to observe, all were either Caucasian or of Hispanic heritage. Best I can say about their escape vehicle is that it had four doors and its front appeared green to me. Got to go. Take care."

And with that Solitaire started running down the alley in the same direction the kidnappers car went. However, wearing the bulky remains of the Reginald Andrews disguise, her pace was far less.

With barely any light to see by, beyond the dim glow of an occasional lit fixture over a receiving dock door, Solitaire reached into a front jacket pocket and pulled out what appeared to be a pair of sunglasses. Yet donning them made everything appear as if it was high noon, for the specially made lenses provided excellent night vision.

Thankfully I was already in the Gulf Coast on other business when Reginald Andrews contacted the website with his plea for help, but I didn't have much time to prepare, let alone scout the terrain earlier this evening. The authorities are bound to have the other end of this alley covered by now, so—

With that Solitaire turned and started ascending the closest fire escape.

Dang! I don't weigh as much as I appear to, yet this disguise makes climbing more difficult, was her silent curse, but the roof was still reached before any cops appeared.

With feet firmly planted on over tarred gravel, Solitaire turned to look back down and saw two sets of flashlight beams coming from different directions about to converge.

They stopped in front of each other below her position. While the officers holding them were relatively stationary and unfortunately out of hearing range, the Clandestine Crusader could easily imagine the conversation's main points. Including where was the alleged Fed?

Solitaire slowly backed away from the edge of the two-story building to prevent anyone from discovering the answer to that question, then viewed the immediate area.

It was a basic tar-gravel roof with traditional air heating and cooling system components. Unfortunately, none of the vents were large enough to use as a potential escape route. There was a structural access point in the middle but, besides not having any lock picks, the building's interior was unknown. *Don't want to trip any burglar alarms, or worse.*

There was another fire escape diagonally opposite, but Solitaire needed to change identities first before taking the chance of descending.

Being a Mistress of Disguise, among her other skills, this was far from Solitaire's first double identity operation. Besides the usual false fingerprint applications, dyed hair underneath balding skin cap and colored contact lenses, other precautions had been taken. She quickly shed the Reginald Andrews costume, revealing another outfit underneath the padded body suit and bulletproof vest.

Male disguises were often necessary between impersonating specific people and throwing enemies off the scent of who was working against them, for most up to anything nefarious usually assumed they were fighting a male opponent.

As she changed, Solitaire thought, *I disguised my voice, but only had time to talk to Andrews and his wife over the phone about their son's kidnapping. While he sounded tired, Reginald said he was clean shaven. His last Internet photo, with a mustache, was almost two years old. So was the enemy's information out of date or is something else going on?*

All the old clothing was now in a pile except for the repurposed belt, shoes and socks, along with the vest and what few accessories could be brought on this mission. There was only one pocket on the tropical print shirt she now displayed, where the sunglasses would be stored. The remaining items were placed in various pockets of the designer pants worn under Andrews' much larger trousers to help Solitaire blend in better with the late-night party scene Miami was famous for.

Briefly raising her legs, Solitaire reached down and opened the magnetic catch that kept each shoe heel in place long enough to remove a plastic vial from a hollowed out space within.

Individually the clear liquid within each container was harmless, but as Solitaire poured them liberally on the clothing pile, they mixed to form a powerful acid that started destroying the Andrews attire.

This isn't what I originally had planned to get out of here, but it's always good to have back up contingencies available.

After tossing the empty vials on top of the dissolving heap to be destroyed too, Solitaire wondered what to do with the bulletproof vest. There wasn't enough acid to even attempt erasing it from existence and the chemical reaction would fizzle out before reaching the roof underneath.

In the end, a plain American quarter was used as a makeshift screwdriver to take off an air vent cover just long enough to hide the vest within its shaft. Solitaire hoped at some point retrieval was possible but, even if discovered, there was no way it could ever be traced back to her.

With the shaft resealed Solitaire was about to check out the other fire escape when two things happened.

She spotted a helicopter in the distance with a search light actively scanning the streets as it flew over as the roof access door started to open.

CHAPTER 3

Wary of the double danger Solitaire hastily searched for shelter, but the closest spot was the blind sides of the building access point in the roof's center. The vent with the bulletproof vest was too short to hide behind and while large enough, the air circulating machinery was in the far corner.

Yet sanctuary was too late to obtain as the door fully opened to reveal a young couple in the throes of an amorous tryst that they hoped was about to turn seriously physical.

"Oh baby. You make me so hot," the woman cooed, rubbing herself against the man.

"Me too," he replied, holding her close.

A couple of inches taller than her, he appeared average and looked in decent physical shape while she was definitely an over bleached bottle blonde with too many artificial fillers.

With no other options available, Solitaire started cautiously making her way toward the exit beyond the couple.

So lost in their moment, she wasn't noticed by either one until within arm's reach of the door, when a loose patch of gravel underfoot announced Solitaire's presence.

"Hey man, what are you doing up here?" the guy demanded to know, moving his face just enough from his now cheek kissing partner to stare at the intruder.

"Don't mind me pal," Solitaire began in yet another male voice. "My date led me up here for some privacy earlier but when I wouldn't pay to play, she beat me to the exit and left me stranded."

A brief glance skyward confirmed the helicopter was still searching the area for at least the getaway car, if not the missing 'Federal Agent' as well. *They can't connect the current me to that unless they find me up here and start asking a bunch of questions I can't answer,* thought Solitaire.

"Why didn't you use one of the fire escapes?" the man wondered, taking a closer look at the stranger.

The false identity was barely in his twenties, just a little over five feet tall with red hair, pale complexion and slim body. A far cry from the much older and heavier Reginald Andrews. "Thought of it, but I've had a bum knee since high school football," Solitaire replied, briefly pointing to the left leg.

"Oh. Sorry to hear that. I—" Then something occurred to the man as he turned to look at his date.

"I don't like the fact that someone else is working my turf, but I'm negotiable," the woman said with a smile, while rubbing a hand across what she could access of her paramour's brown haired chest through his partially unbuttoned shirt. Neither of them thought twice about the other's top completely covering the upper body on such a warm night.

"I'm not," he replied, turning to leave when she stepped between them and the access door.

"Too bad. Wasn't counting on the bonus," the woman said, staring at the disguised Solitaire, "but both of you are going to hand me all the cash you have right now or I'll start screaming rape."

"As if," the man said.

"Hey, it may be two against one, but who do you think the police will believe?" she asked with a smile. "I can say you led me up here under false pretenses and your friend was waiting for us."

"Not going to work," Solitaire replied with a smile of her own.

"Oh? Why not?" the woman asked.

"I can answer that," a new voice replied.

The woman turned and saw a uniformed security guard standing in the open doorway.

"Since we're now officially closed for the night, I just came up here to secure the roof fire exit but heard it all," the guard revealed. "Soon as we get back downstairs and take your picture for our Rogues Gallery, you're banned for life lady!"

"WHAT?" exclaimed the woman in disbelief.

"Club policy. We don't cater to undesirables," the guard explained, staring intently at her while asking, "Do either of you gentlemen care to press charges?"

"Unless you need me to confirm what she said just now, I can't. She isn't the one who stranded me up here," lied Solitaire.

"As long as I never see her again, I'm happy," the woman's intended target answered.

The security guard was about to say something when a voice behind him called out, "Hey Larry. Everything all right up there?"

"Yeah, but get the camera ready. I caught another would be working girl," Larry replied, taking the woman by the arm to escort her downstairs.

+++

The parking lot outside the club had cleared fairly quickly after "Last Call". With the doors locked behind them, the final two patrons stood outside the main entrance. One stared at the lone car much closer to the building than the employees' vehicles at the far end of the property, while the other took discrete glances at the sky whenever possible.

"Hey man, you did me a solid back there. Can I give you a lift somewhere?"

"Appreciate it, but no thanks. I called a cab while you were giving the security guard your statement," Solitaire answered, already planning a covert route back to her Miami safe house.

Of more importance was not seeing any sign of the search helicopter. *I wonder if they caught them?*

"Well, in any event, if you ever need anything," the other man said, handing Solitaire a business card.

"Elias Thompson, Attorney at Law. Impressive. Afraid I'm just Leo Turner, everyday retail sales. No business card," she added with a shrug.

"Hey, as long as it's honest work, there's nothing to be ashamed of."

Solitaire agreed as a cab came into view. "Well, there's my ride. Despite the circumstances it was nice meeting you," Leo said to be polite.

"Same here. Take care," Elias replied as 'Leo' entered the cab and gave the driver directions to the first covert stop on the way to her true destination.

+++

The fare paid cash upon being let off at one of the many apartment complexes in Miami just a few miles from the club.

Solitaire acted like a tenant going home for the night as she started walking deeper into the complex until the cab was out of sight. With that she turned around and walked across the street to the corner bus stop.

It would still be awhile before the first bus of the day even started out on its route, let alone reached this point on its initial run. Yet the magnetic key box hidden under the empty bench was accessible.

With that in hand the Secret Samaritan walked around the corner to another apartment complex a couple of blocks away.

The key was used to open and start a nondescript compact car that had been left on the property earlier that day like any other tenant's vehicle. The path to it had been taken backwards to plant the key before catching a bus elsewhere.

Mobile again, Solitaire took a long, roundabout route to her destination, making sure she wasn't being followed at any point along the way.

+++

After reaching her sanctuary and making sure everything was secured, Solitaire took a long shower to wash out the hair dye and clean up from that night's foray.

Not wanting another military style Meal Ready to Eat that every hideout around the world was well stocked with, she nuked a microwavable Fettuccine Alfredo dinner and poured herself a glass of milk from fresh supplies acquired after reaching Miami before sitting down at a computer terminal to dine and work. Despite surviving another operation, the Discrete Defender knew the overall mission was far from over.

The plea for help from the Andrews family over the website was genuine, yet the whole ransom gig was a set-up from the start. Someone's definitely after Reginald, but does the real Fredrick bear any guilt or is he another potential target? Solitaire wondered while initiating several data searches. *While the same height and basic build, the alley darkness and my lack of prep time were the only reasons that guy's attempt to impersonate him had any success at all.*

I know I didn't have enough time to make the Reginald disguise perfect, but he saw right through my impersonation and I barely said a word. Yet whoever that Fredrick really was called me 'Andrews' and not something more familiar like 'Dad', Solitaire thought, opening a new window to start scanning local news services while awaiting the search results.

Besides needing to confirm the real Fredrick's whereabouts, what also concerns me is that nobody did anything to conceal their identities. Were they that confident about escaping or was leaving no witnesses part of the plan?

Then Solitaire came across a headline she wished wasn't true.

FOUR FOUND DEAD IN ALLEY!

The image that accompanied the article, which basically talked about someone finding a car and the bodies inside as they were reporting to work, showed a vehicle similar in appearance to what she was able to make out of the kidnappers', parked in a different alley only a few miles from the ransom exchange.

No details about the victims other than it being the driver and three passengers, but that's standard procedure pending notifying the next of kin and the fact that it's sketchy information at best in a recently posted online article of breaking news, Solitaire observed, yet something wasn't right. Counting the unseen driver who remained behind the wheel, it was a team of six. *Are two of them still alive? One might have managed to escape despite being injured. The other had to be the shooter, who decided not to share the ransom and split after cutting his partners out of any deal they might have had.*

There was also no mention of the briefcase or its contents, but that could be something the police were withholding for now. Yet Solitaire would have the last laugh financially. One of the demands was no tracking devices hidden within the briefcase. There was no way around not honoring that, for even one on delayed activation would have been detected with the proper scanner. Another was that the entire ransom was to be paid only with Reginald's personal shares of Andrews Aviation.

On such short notice without adequate time to raise the high ransom since the stock was in various bank vaults—another indicator that something wasn't quite right about the whole situation—the falsified bearer bonds she printed would have any kidnapper arrested upon trying to redeem one. *But why did they only want stock?*

Solitaire's thoughts were interrupted by the results of another search.

Fredrick Andrew's last credit card transaction was in Cancun two days ago, confirming what little the family knew of their jet setting son's whereabouts. Did the kidnappers at least know Fredrick wasn't in Miami and try to take advance of the situation or is something else going on? Either way, it will be quicker to attempt tracking down the missing men here than fly there.

With that Solitaire started a discrete data search for gunshot victims receiving treatment within the last few hours. Especially any that might be in police custody.

+++

"Mi amor!" Carol Evans exclaimed, walking into the living room dressed for a new day as a man entered her apartment via his own key. "I was just getting ready for work. How'd it go?"

"Twenty million in Reginald Andrews' personal stock, just like I planned mi Querida," her lover said happily while holding up the ransom briefcase, blissfully unaware of the forgeries inside. He received a warm embrace and a long kiss before being able to speak again. "If all goes according to plan, by the end of the month I'll have reclaimed everything he stole from me."

CHAPTER 4

It was just half past seven that morning when the man walked into one of Miami's many hospitals. After clearing the security checkpoint, he strolled confidently toward the front desk. His appearance was immaculate, even if the suit wasn't actually as top of the line as it first seemed.

"Can I help you?" the main lobby's receptionist on duty asked, turning away from her computer terminal to face the stranger as he placed a leather attaché on the counter.

"Elias Thompson, Attorney at Law," he replied, showing her both his Florida identification and a business card before putting his wallet away. "It's my understanding you might have one of my clients here as a patient. If so, I'd like to see him please."

"Who?" she asked, turning to face her computer again.

"Jacob Marcos."

"Just a second please."

Although he pretended otherwise, Thompson watched closely as keyboard buttons were pressed. A moment later, the lady was about to reveal the results of her data inquiry when two uniformed Miami police officers approached the desk.

"Sir. I'm Officer Milner and this is my partner, Officer Kent. Can we have a moment of your time?" the older looking of the two men asked.

"Certainly," Thompson replied after turning to face them.

"We were wondering why you are inquiring about Jacob Marcos," Kent explained.

"From time to time, attorneys of the firm I work for are assigned pro bono defendants because the owner likes to give back to the community when he can. Anyway, I was awoken from a sound sleep about forty-five minutes ago by someone saying Marcos, who my firm has represented before in some previous but minor encounters with law enforcement, might be down here and possibly in need of legal assistance. Hence, here I am," explained Thompson as innocently as possible.

"Any idea who called you?" Milner inquired.

"Other than it was a male voice that I didn't recognize and that the call was to my work cell instead of my personal one, I'm afraid not."

"Do you know the number they called from?" Kent wondered.

"I checked Caller ID afterward, but all it said was 'Unknown'. Is something wrong?" Thompson asked. "If I have to, I can call a more senior partner to come down and assist me."

"Your client was one of five men shot at point blank range within a car earlier this morning," Milner revealed. "Marcos got lucky though because the bullet meant to kill him was deflected by the cellphone in his shirt pocket just enough to avoid hitting the heart."

"Dang!" Thompson exclaimed. "Did you catch the shooter? Who is it?"

"We're not at liberty to disclose that information at this time," Milner replied.

Thompson figured either the authorities weren't prepared to announce they had a suspect in custody yet or were still looking for the shooter.

Instead, he inquired about seeing Marcos.

"As long as you don't mind one of us accompanying you," Milner said.

"As long as you don't violate attorney-client privilege," was Thompson's response.

Officer Milner stayed behind while his partner escorted Elias Thompson to the Surgical Recovery Ward. Both men were silent on the uneventful journey, yet the attorney's mind was a whirlwind of mental activity, observing everything while pretending not to be looking at anything in particular.

Upon reaching their destination and checking in with the On Duty Nurse there, Officer Kent remained by the entrance as Thompson walked into the small room and approached the foot of the hospital bed Jacob Marcos occupied. While dark skinned, his face looked ashen in the muted hospital light. If not for the white linen cased pillow his head laid upon, his black hair almost blended into the gloom.

"If this is their idea of Stable but Guarded..." the attorney commented, while staring at all the monitors attached to the man lying there. Then he cleared his throat before saying, "Mister Marcos?"

There was no immediate response.

"Señor Marcos?" Thompson said, rephrasing the question.

Barely opening his eyes, the patient replied in a low voice, "S-Si."

"I'm Elias Thompson, Attorney at Law," to which Marcos' eyes widened.

"I can't afford..."

"It's okay. An amigo of yours called my office and said you might need help. I work for free and just want to know what happened to you."

Growing more alert but either unable or unwilling to move, Marcos looked around and spotted the police officer standing in the doorway. "What's he doing here?"

"I'm Officer Kent. You were shot. Almost killed, and we want to catch whoever did it."

"As long as you don't mind one of us accompanying you."

"Bueno. The others? Juan, Chavez, Carlos…" Marcos began.

"I'm afraid you're the only one still alive," Kent told him.

Marcos closed his eyes and being nearer, Thompson noticed a tear begin to form.

"Good amigos," Marcos said.

"Then help us catch who did it. Tell us what you know," requested Kent.

Marcos opened his eyes and stared briefly at the officer again. Then turned to look at the other man.

Thompson nodded that it was okay, so Marcos began by saying, "Mi amigos, we went out to party. Have a good time."

"And did you? Have a good time, that is," the attorney wondered.

"Si. Until Rafael met this guy he knew at our last stop," Marcos replied.

"Who?" Officer Kent asked.

"Don't know name. They seemed okay at first, then the guy started getting mad at Rafael about something. They kept talking even as he followed us back to Juan's car. No spaces left in front of club, so we had to park in rear. Rest of us got in while Rafael rolled down his window to keep talking," recalled the wounded man.

"Where was Rafael sitting?" Kent asked.

"Passenger side, rear. Other end from where I was," answered Marcos. "Juan was about to turn the key so we could all go grab some breakfast together when the guy pulls a gun and starts shooting."

"Can you describe him?" the officer wondered.

"Taller than me and I am… was the biggest. Thin. Dark hair. Real black. Eyes too, but they were always angry looking, even when he wasn't angry," Marcos remembered.

"Based on Marcos' height, the suspect is close to if not taller than six feet. I'll be right back," Kent said, turning to leave so he could report what he just learned.

"Can I have some water, por favor?" Marcos inquired.

"I'll bring it back with me," Kent promised before walking out the door.

Elias Thompson waited to make sure they were truly alone before turning to face Jacob Marcos again. He gave the man a friendly smile before saying in a more menacing tone of voice, "Is what you just said the truth? And what happened to the briefcase with the ransom?"

"W-who are you?" Marcos demanded to know, cowering in the hospital bed the best he could.

"A friend, if you don't lie to me," replied Thompson in the same low, but now a tad more pleasant voice.

"Si," swore Marcos. "Hombre always talking. Grande plans about ruining some other hombre named Andrews. Whoever that is. Hired us for night," he added, after looking to make sure the cop had yet to return.

"You and your amigos were a crew?" While Jacob Hernandez Marcos' criminal record dated back to sealed Juvenile Hall Court cases, the worst he had been charged with as an adult–to date–was petty theft incidents.

"Si. We are, were Los Cuervos. The Crows, but Rafael, our Jefe, said we should always stay low key. We never displayed tats or colors or bragged about jobs. I think he got the idea from that hombre. Anyway, that's how we lasted for so long, until..."

"What did happen in the car?"

"Hombre was sitting where I said Rafael was. Rafael was actually on his left. Said we were doing his amigo a favor helping out on that job. Crowded in back with quarto. Metal case with money in his lap, but mad that real Andrews wasn't there. How he knew, I have no idea," swore Marcos.

"Go on," urged Thompson, not knowing how much longer their solitude would last.

"We went straight to that alley after leaving first one. Juan parked and all was quiet for a bit, but I could see hombre still angry when Carlos asked what our share was going to be. That's when he turned on us and started shooting. Thought I was dying when I saw him take the money and run. Don't know where."

"What else can you tell me about him?" Thompson asked.

"I honestly don't know his name, but hombre not fully Americano, yet not all Hispanic either. I—"

Then suddenly a nurse walked into the room, pushing a waist high cart. "Hola Señor Marcos. I'm Susanna and I'll be your nurse for today. The nice police officer said you were thirsty. I've got some water and medication for you, but first I have to check your vitals."

"And that's my cue to leave," announced the attorney in his normal voice as he turned to depart. "I hope you get well soon."

"Gracias," Marcos replied, watching the doorway long after Thompson left the room.

+++

In the hallway, attorney and police officer reunited.

"How much of his story do you believe?" Officer Kent asked.

"I've never met Jacob Marcos before today, so only the part about who shot him," admitted Thompson. "Why?"

"Our early ballistics results show the shooter's assault angle puts him physically *inside* the car and not outside it," revealed Kent. "Despite its sketchiness, hopefully the description Marcos gave us pans out. How does your firm plan to proceed?"

"I report what happened here back to my superior and we wait to see if you file any charges against Marcos or if he decides to sue the shooter after you catch him. Either way, I'm going to let someone else handle the matter from this point on. I've got a full case load as it is and no wiggle room for extra work at the moment."

"Okay," Kent replied, before saying goodbye.

With that Elias Thompson left the Surgical Recovery Ward and waved to Officer Milner at the front Security Desk on his way out of the hospital.

Walking to the adjacent municipal parking garage, it was a disguised Solitaire who started ascending to the upper levels.

Posing as Thompson was the quickest opportunity I could create on short notice after finding a possible gunshot suspect. I'm sure Milner checked out his credentials while I was upstairs but thankfully the real attorney is either still home or already at his office for the day, because a quick background check revealed his firm doesn't do pro bono work, Solitaire thought. *I must admit the receptionist is good at her job because unless there was a hidden emergency icon on the computer screen, I never saw her do anything to alert Security.*

Solitaire waited patiently for the garage's passenger elevator. Once inside, the car buttons were pressed for all the remaining floors.

The only risky part was if the officers tried to detain me or insisted on seeing a senior attorney. Then Thompson would have bowed out somehow that didn't get the real one into trouble while I searched for answers elsewhere, or they waited for someone who would never appear.

When the lift stopped on three, having already ascertained where the security camera was, it appeared as if Elias Thompson left the elevator.

Instead, the Clandestine Crusader covertly went to the car's opposite corner out of surveillance range and quickly turned the reversible men's jacket she was wearing inside out to present its alternate exterior before stashing the brown wig in the briefcase to display her own natural, pixie short hair.

When the elevator stopped on four, a total stranger got out and walked to a different automobile than the one Solitaire used earlier.

While the police apparently don't know about the false ransom exchange and the shooter's dual heritage, I'll have to let them handle this matter for now while I go to Cancun and make sure the real Fredrick Andrews is alive and well.

CHAPTER 5

C arol Evans' lover and co-conspirator was asleep in her queen size bed when his cellphone chimed.

Knowing it wasn't the preset wake up alarm, he groggily reached for it off her nightstand, glanced at the Caller ID and said "Hola."

"Boss, we've got a problem," the man on the other end announced without any preamble.

"Is our guest—"

"He's resting comfortably but your lawyer called. His courier is in the hospital after being ambushed on the way here."

"Maldición," his superior cursed, while sitting up in the bed. "Who—"

"Local bandidos. They took everything he had, including his car and briefcase."

"Por qué—"

"The courier says he was just another target to them. In the wrong place at the wrong time with them having no idea of who he was or his connection to us. However, because you want the lawyer to handle everything privately, it's going to take at least a day before he can replace the documents and make arrangements for another discrete courier."

"Aye…" *First a fake Andrews and now this. At least Rafael never knew who I really am, so I finally got rid of those annoying Crows.* The man paused to think things over before asking, "Is your position secure?"

"I don't like staying in one place for so long, but as long as our host's credit is good…"

"It is. For now," he replied, getting out of bed. "Send some men you can spare to find and teach those ladrones a lesson they'll remember for what little is left of their miserable lives. Otherwise stay there until the new papers arrive. I want them signed and officially processed before you carry out the rest of my orders concerning our guest."

"Si," the man acknowledged before ending the call.

After using Evans' bathroom, he returned to his lover's bed but instead of falling back asleep, he decided to check on other matters first.

+++

Carol Evans was working at her computer when the cellphone secretly laying in her lap, hidden from view by the desk, quietly vibrated to signal receipt of an incoming text. Pausing from her task to discretely read the message, all she saw displayed were three question marks from an allegedly unknown sender but knew who and what it meant.

She secured the computer and left the BACK SOON sign prominently on her desk after switching the office phone over to the building's main operator to answer in case of an incoming call while away. Then Evans rose and discretely carried the phone with her to the nearby ladies' room.

After making sure she was totally alone within the facility, Carol leaned against the basin counter with her back to the oversized wall mirror to keep an eye on the entrance before calling a number not programmed into her phone but committed to memory.

"Hi. I was sitting at my desk, typing up the notes from this morning's board meeting. I'll have the formal report ready to distribute later this afternoon and will make sure you get a copy," she said in a low voice.

"Good. Anything of note?" her boyfriend asked.

"Other than Marketing arguing with Research and Development again over potential commercial names for the prototype once it's publicly available, no," she answered. "Even if I'm right and Ariel does suspect anything, the subject was never brought up in the meeting. The test is still planned for 0800 the day after tomorrow. I'll be flying out with her in the morning to oversee the final preparations. Both the ones she wants and yours."

"Then we still have tonight?" he asked.

"Si," Carol happily replied.

"Bueno. I'm still at your place. See you then," he promised before ending the call.

Laying back in her bed, the man stared at the ceiling and pondered the future. *She's a nice señorita. Too bad there can be no loose ends when all of this is over.*

+++

Although only officially in existence since 1970, Cancun has become a major tourist attraction of both Mexico and the Caribbean. Over one million people actually called the coastal city home, while many more maintained residences that were only used a couple of weeks each year at most.

"Señorita Frieda, what a pleasant surprise," the hacienda's majordomo said as he greeted the woman. While his attire was akin to what one would expect for a butler, the suit was all white to accommodate local weather and customs with just the tie adding a splash of color, compared to the more traditional black hued wardrobe a man in his position usually wore.

"Hola Fernando. It's nice to see you again too," the long blonde-haired woman replied as she walked through the front door with a matching suitcase in each hand and a briefcase tucked under her left arm.

"Here, let me help," Fernando offered, taking the suitcase on her right. "We have not seen any of the Daye familia in weeks, but we only have the pleasure of your company this time?"

"Afraid so. My sister Virginia is in California overseeing a new ecological reclamation program on the Pacific Coast. The rest of the family is all over the world as usual, but when my business in Mexico City ended sooner than expected, I realized it's been ages since I had a vacation, let alone came back here." *The Dayes may be rich, but they're certainly not idle.*

"Well, on behalf of Cancun, the rest of the household staff and myself, it is a pleasure to see you again. Yet I must apologize. We received no advance word of your arrival until the Seguridad announced your presence at the front gate. Ramone is off today, but I would have gladly gotten you from the airport myself, had I known," the gray-haired Hispanic gentleman added, watching the taxi pull away as he secured the entrance.

"It's okay Fernando," replied Frieda, while switching the briefcase to her now free hand. "As usual, the casa looks perfect. My compliments to you and the staff," she added, taking in her surroundings. If the front foyer and living room behind the man who greeted her were any indication, the house was spacious. Tastefully decorated in local décor, it appeared more like the modest dwelling of an urban family than the part time residence of a rich one. Only the perimeter fencing and the guards patrolling the multi-acre property said otherwise.

"Gracias. I shall pass along your compliment," Fernando replied, while taking the other suitcase. "I trust everything has been going well since I have seen you last?" he asked, turning to lead his mistress to her bedroom.

"Si. The Daye family enterprises thrive, and the Foundation's charitable works are helping millions around the world."

"That's good. Shall I have Consuela at least prepare something for you to snack on, if not an actual meal?" the Major Domo wondered, leading the way upstairs.

"No, but I would appreciate some agua. It's been a long flight and I'm going to have a siesta first," the lady requested as Fernando opened the door of their destination.

"Si. Uno momento, por favor." With that he set the bags down inside the room by the door and turned to leave.

Frieda Daye looked around as she walked over to the desk in one corner and set the briefcase on its work surface. A big screen television sat on a stand; its screen angled toward a king sized bed with a matching night stand on either side. Two other doors indicated the presence of a walk-in closet and private bath.

Wasn't sure what to expect, but this room's more like being in a hotel suite than the stuff of champagne wishes and caviar dreams.

She sat at the desk and pulled a computer tablet out of the briefcase. Booting it up was the only task accomplished as the sound of footsteps on the hallway's hardwood floor heralded someone approaching the still open bedroom door.

"Oh, Señorita Daye, just look at you," a matronly woman said with a broad smile as she walked in, carrying a small tray with both hands. Upon it was a sealed, clear plastic pitcher full of water and ice cubes with a glass sitting upside down on a coaster next to it. "Your parents must be very proud of the woman you've become," the lady added.

"They are, and how are your children Consuela?" Frieda asked, rising to take the tray from her.

"Bueno. Julio just entered university and Carlita will be graduating high school next year," the head cook answered proudly.

"Grande," Frieda replied, setting the tray down on the desk. *The Dayes keep the staff employed year round so they're always earning a steady paycheck and discretely help out with their other needs when necessary.* "And your husband?"

"Fine. With his green thumb he loves working on the grounds around here but still hopes to become an abuelo someday. Yet I keep telling him our kids need to establish their own lives before becoming parents themselves."

"Si. Mi Madre is always wondering when I might find someone too."

"I can imagine. Anyway, Fernando wanted me to tell you that transportation shall be available when needed and whenever you're hungry, you just let me know and I'll fix something really deliciosa," Consuela promised. With that she smiled and left the room, closing the door behind her.

Frieda Daye waited a moment to make sure the lady was gone before locking the door. Then she sat down at the desk and poured herself a drink before entering data.

Would have been here sooner, but besides the flight delays because of that tropical storm in the Gulf of Mexico, I had to double check where all the Dayes really were right now. While this was the most advantageous disguise available, it wouldn't do to come waltzing in portraying someone already here, thought Solitaire.

The safe house for this area is only a few miles from here. Once a local data search either confirms or updates the results of the one I conducted before leaving Miami, I'll scout Fredrick Andrews' last known location for either him or clues to where he might be now and follow the trail from there.

+++

The moment they returned to her apartment from an extravagant meal at one of Miami's finer restaurants, Carol Evans and her boyfriend went straight to the bedroom, but not for sleep.

She once again couldn't help noticing they were a study in contrasts. César Fernandez was in his late twenties. Handsome, tall and skinny with smoldering black eyes and hair as dark as a starless night.

While being shorter wasn't a bad thing, Carol knew her looks were rather plain but far from ugly. Yet her long locks were still like a bright burning fire and her eyes akin to a peaceful forest. Being too near the big Four-Oh worried her at times, but it didn't slow Evans down.

Carol realized a long-term relationship, let alone matrimony, wasn't in her future because she knew the real reason César had expressed any interest in her. They shared a common objective, and he thought of her as just a means to an end. Yet two could play that game, and the sex was good.

After several vigorous dances of the 'horizontal mambo', Carol asked "Everything ready on your end?"

"Si. This mission is too important to trust to underlings and it's too risky for us to fly, so my men and I will start out in the van tomorrow morning. We'll take turns driving and should be in position before the demonstration starts," César replied, while putting an arm around her.

"Good," Carol said, nestling next to him. "You have your issues against the Andrews family and I have mine. Separately they think we're beneath their notice but together, they won't know what hit them."

And neither will you when the time comes, she silently added while kissing César again.

+++

It was well after ten the next morning when the lowly maid pushed her cleaning cart across the industrial carpeting of the Hotel Paradiso's eighth floor. Several suite doors had 'Do Not Disturb' signs on display, their tenants asleep after heartily enjoying Cancun's rich night life. The rest either showed 'Maid Service Requested' or no sign at all as their occupants were out and about on the new day's tourist agendas. They would all be serviced eventually, but standard procedure was to start at the far end and work back toward the elevators, which is why she stopped in front of room 810. A corner suite, the even numbered accommodations faced the crystal blue waters of the Caribbean while the odds viewed the mainland. Yet that didn't matter to her as the door's electronic reader checked the digital chip in her employee pass card. Once access was granted, she entered cart first.

This room was like all the others on the lower floors since the more deluxe suites were not available until the tenth. A brief foyer with bathroom entrance on the side as two King size beds with a night table between them faced twin waist high dressers and a wall mounted television in the open area beyond the beds' foot boards.

The room didn't look too messy. Normally she would be in, done and out within a half hour at the most.

However two things stopped the maid in her tracks.

Seeing the man wearing only underwear tied by thick ropes to the far bed with a gag in his mouth was bad enough.

The fully dressed man standing at the front edge of the cleaning cart holding a gun pointed at her head was another matter.

CHAPTER 6

"What the hell are you doing here?" the man with the gun shouted angrily.

"H-here to clean room," the maid replied in English with a thick Hispanic accent, both scared and stating the obvious.

"We don't want the room cleaned," announced another voice as suddenly the door was closed behind her, trapping the lady between two armed men. Except for the empty weapon holsters over their left shoulders, they were both dressed like causal tourists in light weight long pants and tropical print short sleeve shirts. Two jackets were laid across the foot of the unoccupied bed.

"Then you should have hung sign," the maid said, unsure which gunman to look at and what they were going to do with her. With their tanned skin, well-groomed hair and neatly trimmed mustaches, both appeared to be local hombres of some means. Yet unlike her, they spoke English perfectly without a hint of any accent.

"We did," replied the man by the door.

"Saw no sign," she repeated.

"Keep an eye on her," ordered the one closer to the door as he turned to check.

The man in front of the maid simply nodded. The gun never once moved from its target as he sat confidently on the edge of the waist high dresser behind him, staring at her like a bug he wanted to squish.

"She's right. It's gone," the other announced a moment later, securing the door in the process.

"No sign," the maid repeated, still scared but a tad more confident.

"What are we going to do with her?" asked the first man.

"Damned if I know. Tie her up until we can ask the boss?"

"Who hasn't called us since I had to call him," the other reminded his partner. "If it wasn't for the courier being due later today, I'd say we cut our loses and get out while we can. After all, the boss did say no witnesses and I seriously doubt anyone will miss this old hag," he added, a slur against the maid's gray hair, wrinkled face and hands.

With that the man stood and aimed the gun at her chest instead of head this time.

While never completely living up to their name, the fact both weapons had a silencer attached to their muzzles indicated that murder could be successfully committed, undetected by anyone who might be in the neighboring suites.

"MI DIOS!" the maid shouted.

"Kidnapping is one thing, but I didn't sign up for any killing," the man by the door complained.

"I have no problem with it," his partner coldly commented, finger steady upon the trigger. *And I'll gladly kill you too if I have to listen to you whine much longer.*

"Let's at least tie her up until we either do hear from the boss or have to take matters into our own hands."

"That I can live with, for now," the other finally said, although he never lowered his weapon.

"Okay Señora, get moving," said the one behind her as he came closer, urging her further into the room.

"Si," the maid agreed, before elbowing the man in the gut with her right arm while pushing the cleaning cart with her left as hard as she could into the other.

There were two satisfying 'oofs,' but the maid didn't stop as she now grabbed the man behind her by his gun hand with both arms.

Catching him off guard, she managed to swing him around into the cleaning cart, pushing it into his partner again even harder than before. The first time that man was only knocked against the waist high dresser. Now his legs were momentarily pinned as he unwillingly fell back upon the fixture, further delaying his recovery from the blows.

Yet the other one never hesitated to raise his gun. Whether to shoot or club the maid with it was a moot point as her left hand grabbed his wrist to keep the weapon at bay long enough for her right fist to punch the man in the windpipe.

He gasped for air and fell toward the corner of the closest bed as she took and threw the gun into the cleaning cart's small water bucket while grabbing the mop from it in one fluid motion.

The wet strands went straight into the first man's face as he started to free himself from between cart and dresser. Then the mop was spun around and its wooden handle slammed into his wrist.

Reluctantly releasing the weapon, he managed to swing his left fist instead of trying to ease his aches, only to feel the blunt end of the handle plunge into his gut.

As he bent over in pain, a hard karate chop to the carotid artery finished the job as the man fell unconscious toward the suite's rich pile carpeting.

Dazed and still gasping for breath, his partner managed to rise and started staggering toward the door in hopeful escape, but it was not to be as the maid grabbed hold of his hair and slammed him head first into the wall on their right.

There was now a noticeable dent in the painted plaster as the unconscious opponent slumped to the floor.

After making sure the other weapon joined the first in the mop bucket, the maid reached for the portable tray holding cleaning supplies and lifted it up just long enough to retrieve the knife hidden underneath.

With a speed far faster than one would think an elderly lady capable of, she rushed over to the far bed.

The man lying there looked similar to the pretender in the Miami alley only in regards to height and body frame. Six feet tall and relatively skinny, but not as muscular with a bit of excess weight around the middle from living a rich life. There was several days worth of unshaven beard on his face, which matched his dark brown hair. A color that black could pass for in an unlit alley.

"Fredrick Andrews?" the maid asked in a noticeably different female voice, to which he vigorously started nodding his head affirmatively.

With that the disguised Solitaire began cutting him loose.

"Th-thanks. W-who are you?" Andrews wondered as soon as a hand was free so he could remove the gag from his mouth.

"Your parents hired me to find you," was her only response.

"The ransom?"

"Your parents barely had enough time to collect the money, but it was paid. Yet when no word arrived of your whereabouts, I tracked you down."

"What about the jerk who—"

"All that will be taken care of," advised Solitaire. "What's more important right now is are you all right? Can you walk?"

"Not sure yet," he answered, managing to sit up as the 'maid' started cutting the bonds at his ankles. "Except for bathroom trips and meals, I've been attached to this bed for a couple of days now. My captors have been enjoying full room service on my dime while the most I get any meal has been cold cereal or sandwiches."

"What was all that about a courier?" Solitaire asked.

"Your guess is as good as mine. I'm surprised they didn't kill me after they got the ransom."

"Where are your clothes?"

"Hopefully in the dresser," replied Fredrick. "Last thing I remember is coming in here with a sexy Señorita and then waking up the way you found me with those two jerks."

"The lady was probably in on it," she surmised, gathering the rope cords while Andrews rubbed his sore wrists and ankles. "You can tell the authorities all about it when we reach the American Consulate. Get dressed as fast as you can, but don't bother packing anything except identification and don't leave this room without me."

With that Solitaire took the cut ropes and used them to bind the unconscious men so their hands and feet were secured behind their backs. A couple of unsoiled cleaning rags served as makeshift gags. She then went to the cart and retrieved a sealed plastic bag from the bottom of the otherwise empty trash bag before locking herself in the bathroom.

Fredrick Andrews did his best to comply with her request, dressing in the first viable outfit he could piece together. "Damn it! Half my clothes, all the better stuff, are missing. Yet I've never seen any of these creeps wearing them."

He was still looking through the drawers when a noise behind him caught his attention. "I'm almost ready," he began, not bothering to turn around. "For some reason I'm missing my luggage and all my more formal wear, hence the beach outfit," Fredrick said, explaining the tropical print shorts with matching shirt and a pair of sandals. "I did find my wallet, but all my credit cards and cash are also gone. My watch and University Class Ring too. At least I still have my United States ID, Passport and Travel Visa."

"Good, then let's get going," a younger and far different female voice replied.

Fredrick looked up from the open drawer. The woman he saw now was a far cry from the pale, blue eyed old maid who rescued him.

She was a dark-haired beauty with big brown eyes about a head shorter than he was. Fredrick had yet to turn twenty-five, so she couldn't be more than in her late twenties at most. The figure in the light weight but full-length sun dress was much more flattering too. The large tote bag slung over one shoulder seemed appropriate with that outfit, but "Sneakers?" he asked, glancing at her feet.

"Completes the tourist disguise," was Solitaire's only response.

A wig, along with changing clothes and colored contact lenses was easy enough. The borrowed maid outfit was tossed on top of the cleaning cart. Solitaire's knife and unneeded lock picks were now under the false bottom of the tote. A camera and other sightseeing supplies, along with a few 'extras' in case they were needed, sat on top.

Being only temporary, the maid's hair coloring was water soluble, yet removing the washable aging makeup from the exposed parts of her skin took longer than expected. *Gonna have to work on that,* the Clandestine Crusader mused. The false fingerprint applications were still the ones she had donned before entering the Hotel Paradiso, who owned the cart. That would stay in the room now that she had removed all her stuff from it.

"What should I call you?" he wanted to know.

"What's in a name?" Solitaire replied, quoting Shakespeare.

"A rose by any other name would smell as sweet," he answered, completing the quote from *Romeo and Juliet.* "Then lead on fair Juliet," Fredrick added.

As the suite door closed behind them, Solitaire put the missing 'DO NOT DISTURB' sign back in place.

On their way down the corridor to the elevators, Fredrick inquired what time it was.

"Almost noon. Why?" Solitaire asked, glancing at her inexpensive wristwatch.

"We need to hurry! There's been four of these jerks keeping me company in teams of two and it's almost time for the shift change!" exclaimed Andrews as the elevator dinged that the car had arrived before either of them could press the call button.

CHAPTER 7

With any elevator operating system, there are a few crucial seconds between the alert signal's chime and the car doors actually opening to allow anyone waiting time to step back and give disembarking passengers a chance to leave.

In that brief moment, Solitaire reached within the tote bag and palmed what looked like an innocent small canister of breath spray.

Yet as the doors started to open she was spun around and, with back pressed literally against the wall space between the dual elevators, Fredrick Andrews kissed her.

Solitaire's eyes widened in shock as her body tensed. She fought her self-defense instinct to shove Andrews away as two men, dressed similarly to those left in the hotel suite, got off the lift and started walking past them without a second thought about the couple.

Or so they both hoped.

The first one did, intent upon heading toward their destination.

The second had just taken a step past Andrews when it occurred to him something wasn't quite right. "¿Qué—" he began to say, turning to face the couple.

Solitaire started to break away from Fredrick, prepared to handle the situation, when Andrews' spun around and hit the man as hard and fast as he could with his right fist.

There was the personally satisfying sound of knuckles colliding against jaw as the target staggered back from the blow. Yet Fredrick didn't stop and hit the man right in the gut. "You dare hold me hostage, you—" Days of pent-up anger bubbled over as he gave into the growing fury and continued attacking one of his kidnappers.

The other man turned at the noise as his right hand started instinctively reaching into the left side of the jacket he wore.

Hoping Andrews could handle his opponent, Solitaire rushed to close the short gap between herself and the other kidnapper.

"Perdóneme," she began. "¿Conoces el camino a San José?"

He turned toward her, completely caught off guard between seeing a good looking señorita and being asked such an inane question, with hand still in jacket.

Solitaire pushed the button down on the small canister and spritzed the man right between the eyes with pepper spray.

Seriously blinded by the burning liquid searing sensitive optical tissue, he started rubbing and trying to clear his eyes with both hands. Gravity finished pulling the gun out of the interior holster as it fell to the floor's industrial carpet.

Solitaire never hesitated to raise her right leg and kick her opponent between his legs. The man doubled over in even more intense pain, which left him vulnerable to a two-fisted blow against the back of the neck. He hit the floor head first, the impact completing his journey to unconsciousness.

The Mistress of Disguise then turned and was disgusted to see Fredrick still beating upon his adversary, despite the fact the other man was clearly down on the floor and out of the fight.

"Stop!" she said in a commanding voice only loud enough for Andrews to hear.

Fredrick turned his head and stared at her. Then he looked down and realized what happened. "I-I swear, I'm usually not like this. But after being held for so long... Besides, he's wearing my watch."

"We'll discuss it later," she said in a scolding tone. "Right now we've got to secure these two and get going," Solitaire reminded him.

"Where? Back in the suite?" Andrews asked, while reclaiming his property.

"No. That'd take too long and we risk someone possibly seeing us. The

"Right now we've got to secure these two and get going."

Custodian's Closet is closer, around the corner across from the elevators. Grab his arms," she instructed while reaching for the man's legs.

Although the cleaning cart was still within Suite 810 it was a small space, forcing them to leave the sleeping villains in sitting positions. Their backs were against opposing walls with one man's legs on top of the other's. Their guns were tossed in the room's small mop sink, though there was no time to fill it and nothing within the closet to tie the kidnappers up with.

Solitaire closed the door and as they walked back to the elevator, Fredrick asked, "Did I hear you say something to your guy while we were fighting?"

"Si. ¿Conoces el camino a San José?"

"Wait. You asked him 'Do you know the way to San Jose?'" Andrews wanted to know while she pushed the call button. Having not been summoned since the kidnappers disembarked, the elevator doors instantly opened.

"Why not? The distraction worked," Solitaire said in return as she hummed a few bars of the song.

Entering the elevator, Solitaire stood by the controls and turned to face Andrews. "Now then, I totally understand your anger, but it isn't honorable to kick a man when he can no longer defend himself."

"I—" Fredrick began, following her inside.

"I only fight in self defense and know when an opponent's had enough." *No point in muddying the issue with how far I'd actually go if lives were on the line*, she thought, while pushing the ground floor button. "Another thing. Never kiss someone without their permission," Solitaire added, before punching him in the arm.

"Ow. You're stronger than you look," Andrews complained, while rubbing the now sore spot.

"Thanks," she replied as the elevator began its descent.

"You are good looking. I'm sure plenty of guys hit on you as it is, so I apologize," Fredrick sincerely said. Then, as the floor indicator changed from six to five he asked, "Are you married?"

"Si." *To my job*, Solitaire silently added.

"I didn't see a ring. I always look for a ring before—"

"It doesn't go with the disguise and before you ask any more questions, my private life is just that. Private." *Although you're not a bad kisser Fredrick Andrews.*

+++

The rest of the elevator ride to the Hotel Paradiso's luxurious lobby was silent and uneventful.

The two crossed the spacious foyer together like a couple of tourists anxious to see the sights, but Solitaire insisted on a brief stop at the front desk first.

"Excuse me, Señor?" she began with a bright smile at the man behind the counter.

"Si Señorita. How may I help you?" the hotel employee asked.

"My boyfriend and I are in Suite 808 and as we were getting ready to leave, we heard some funny noises coming from 810."

"Oh?" the clerk said, wondering what was going on.

"Yes, and as we were getting on the elevator to leave and go sightseeing for the day, it looked like someone was trying to steal from your janitor's closet," Solitaire added.

Fredrick couldn't keep himself from smiling as the clerk asked, "Really? Can you describe this person?"

"Only the back of a man in a dark suit standing in the open doorway," she replied.

"I'll have someone look into both incidents immediately," promised the clerk.

"Gracias," Solitaire said with a smile before taking Andrews by the arm and leading him outside into the warm Cancun sun.

"Man, it's bright out here," Fredrick complained, raising one hand to shield his eyes as they tried adjusting to the sunlight. "Those bums kept the curtains closed the whole time they had me, so the only way I could even guess whether it was day or night depended upon who was in the room with me and what was on television."

"I figured that was possible. Here," Solitaire said, handing him a spare pair of sunglasses from the tote bag as she donned hers.

"Gracias. Nice trick with the clerk. I hope those jerks get what's coming to them."

"Me too."

"Where's your ride?" he asked, following her.

"Over here," she replied, leading them to the far corner of the parking lot's public area.

"This is a car?" he asked, nearing the passenger side of a small two door conveyance with a bright blue body. "Where's the rest of it?" Andrews wondered, noting the hatch back and small open storage space behind the front seats.

"Don't knock my micro compact," Solitaire replied, while pressing the button on the key fob to open the vehicle. "In part because of not having a back seat, let alone an official trunk, it gets almost forty miles to a gallon."

"Really?" Fredrick said in disbelief as he got inside and secured his seat belt.

"Hybrid engine," Solitaire explained as she checked her rear-view mirror before starting the car to back out of the parking space. After a few seconds in motion, the telltale noise of the doors self-securing themselves could be heard as she changed gears to pull forward and started a slow cruise toward the exit and the main road.

However their journey was cut short as another car pulled out in front of them.

Solitaire managed to stop quickly enough to avoid colliding with the red four door roadblock, which caused its passenger to emerge from the vehicle with a gun pointed at them.

CHAPTER 8

"Don't touch anything. Do exactly what I say when I say it and absolutely nothing else," Solitaire ordered Andrews in a stern voice before telling him to slowly raise his hands as if surrendering, but to stay within the vehicle.

Fredrick complied but didn't say anything about his companion barely raising hers in the process, let alone that the engine was still running.

Upon seeing the gesture, the gunman smiled and motioned with the weapon in his right hand to indicate he wanted them out of the car.

Solitaire looked like she was about to comply when suddenly the vehicle started backing away.

Her last glance of the now angry man showed him shouting something to whoever his driver was. Checking the dashboard console monitor display from the car's rear view camera, Solitaire quickly drove backwards into the parking space she had just left without hitting the automobiles on either side. Then she switched gears and pulled out in the opposite direction before their opponents could catch up.

"Friends of yours?" she asked, noting they were being pursued. The other car's image was now in both vehicle's mirrors and the monitor display. "Don't bothering answering. It was a rhetorical question."

As they reached the end of the lane, Solitaire turned sharply right before another right took them onto the next aisle.

Their tires screeched in protest as the kidnappers' larger automobile almost spun into parked cars trying to make the turns at a higher rate of speed than the posted parking lot warning signs recommended. Although less maneuverable than the micro compact, the four-door sedan managed to get behind them again in seconds.

"Hang on!" Solitaire warned Andrews. The best he could do was brace himself between the dashboard and the passenger door frame as she suddenly turned left onto the pedestrian crosswalk that bisected the large section of parking lot they were in.

The pursuing car slammed on its brakes. Unable to directly follow, the frustrated driver watched the small blue auto go down the striped walkway for several meters before turning left onto the aisle after the next one. The driver then threw his car into reverse and drove backwards to the last intersection in order to change course and hopefully catch their quarry.

However, Solitaire only went down the new aisle just long enough to disappear from sight. Upon figuring the kidnappers had chosen a course of action, she backed her car up and traveled down the pedestrian pathway again to its end and turned left at the last aisle to resume her original course.

With no roadblocks to deter them this time, Solitaire exited the hotel's parking lot. Now on Bulevar Kukulcan, Andrews watched her push a button below the car's built-in monitor that changed the display.

The rear camera view was now consolidated to the right half of the screen as a map appeared on the left-hand side. He soon figured out that the small green dot at the bottom of that was them as Solitaire carefully weaved her way in and out of traffic on their side of the divided, four lane boulevard named after the fabled feathered serpent of Mayan mythology.

"Depending upon the other driver's skills, this will only buy us a few minutes at best, so we better make the most of it," Solitaire said, pushing her right foot down on the gas pedal until the micro compact was skirting the posted kilometer speed limit. "If those guys are that determined to catch us, they'll soon figure out we managed to leave and try finding us again," she warned Fredrick. "Other than our new playmates, did you notice anyone different among your caretakers back at the hotel?"

"No. Yet I honestly thought there were only four of them in teams of two," Andrews said by way of apology.

"Your credit card activity for the last couple of days only showed charges for Suite 810, but if they were taking turns watching you, it makes sense that the off-duty ones had to be staying somewhere else. However, this does pose some new questions."

"Like what?"

"I'm not sure if it's strictly professional or a personal matter, but someone is obviously waging a vendetta against your father. They definitely have some pretty deep pockets to not only employ at least six men and that 'lady' who seduced you here in Cancun, but another group in Miami where the ransom exchange went down," Solitaire deduced, not mentioning the assassination attempt against Reginald Andrews.

"I know Dad has plenty of business rivals, but I'm shocked anyone would go this far to get a heads up on their competition."

"With all that stuff about Megaplex that's been in the news lately?" Solitaire said in disbelief. "Anything going on business wise that this might be a result of?"

"Not that I'm aware of. My sister Ariel actually runs Andrews Aviation. I'm just a major shareholder and a private, as needed trouble shooter she can trust. Which is why I was down here to begin with."

"Oh?"

"She asked me to check out some invoice discrepancies among our clients. Otherwise, I'm not as involved as Dad wishes I—" Then Fredrick stopped to look at the screen again before saying, "Our tail's back."

"Took them a little longer than I thought it would, but it didn't require a genius to figure out we'd be headed for the American Consulate," Solitaire realized, as Fredrick watched the split screen.

The right-hand side now showed the other car closing the distance between them live as the map on the left continued displaying their green dot traveling down the boulevard.

They were in the far left-hand lane as Solitaire spoke. "It's pretty much a direct route from the hotel. We'll pass the Canadian Consular, or Consulate if you prefer, on our right before reaching the United States one on our left. There's still several kilometers to travel before then though, but that doesn't mean we can't do a little sightseeing along the way."

Andrews saw her signal to make a left turn at the intersection they were about to cross. The sedan behind them did the same.

Both vehicles started to turn with the light, but at the last second Solitaire made a complete U-turn to resume her previous course, leaving the other car stuck in the middle of the intersection as its driver anxiously tried to avoid a collision.

"Warn a guy, would you Juliet?" Fredrick protested, bracing himself within the car's interior the best he could. "I'm glad you're driving though. Don't think I'd have the stomach for it."

Solitaire's only reply was a sly smile as she pushed a button to give the rear-view camera display full use of the monitor again.

Despite the closed windows and running air conditioner, the sounds of honking horns, screeching brakes and near misses were heard in relation to the visual image. Yet both were uncertain of there being an actual crash.

Whatever happened, there was currently no sign of the other vehicle.

"Better run while the running's good," Solitaire observed, stepping down on the gas pedal once more. "If they can, they'll be on our six again soon."

Fredrick turned to look at her. "I've got to apologize. This car is better than I first thought."

"It's served me well." *At least, whenever me or any of my predecessors have been in Cancun,* she silently added.

A couple of more blocks were quickly recorded on the odometer before Fredrick announced, "They're behind us again."

As the red sedan's image grew larger on the monitor screen, the micro compact's occupants could see a little damage to its front end, including the car now missing the passenger side headlight, but it obviously was still able to travel.

"I'm skirting the speed limit to not attract attention, so they've got to be going at least a good ten kilometers over it to be back here so soon."

Fredrick watched her push another button on the console, but the only result was a totally white screen briefly appearing before returning to its original presentation.

"No police in the immediate area," she observed before narrowly skirting a traffic light as it changed from yellow to red.

Their car made it across the intersection before the light favored the other road. The sedan's illegal crossing heralded several honking horns accompanying oncoming traffic having to abruptly stop.

Solitaire kept driving as Andrews' attention was split between the monitor and their rear windshield.

"They're almost bumper to bumper with us!" he announced, bracing himself in the belief that the other car was going to attempt ramming them.

Instead, there seemed to be an anti-climatic noise, as if a pebble hit the hatchback windshield.

Fredrick looked around, trying to identify the source, then realized the truth. "They're shooting at us!" he shouted, as the sedan passenger leaned out his open window far enough to aim and fire his weapon again.

"Don't worry. The tires are puncture proof. The body's armored and the glass is bulletproof," Solitaire calmly announced. "The extra weight is why I don't get as much mileage per tank as the manufacturer claims, but what this car lacks there it makes up for in horsepower," she added, fully stomping her foot on the gas pedal.

Her passenger was shocked at the sudden acceleration as they sped even faster down the boulevard. "You've been holding back?"

"Yeah, but only because I had to, not because I wanted to. While we have local plates instead of the special ones issued to tourist transportation to blend in better, the Policía take a dim view of law breakers in their country and none of us can afford to be arrested. Especially those two," Solitaire added as the ping of another bullet failing to pierce the car was heard. "They really want at least you, and I'm not willing to bet on whether it's dead or alive."

Andrews grew sick at that thought as she pressed the same button from earlier, but once more only the white screen momentarily appeared.

"Dang. Still no police nearby," was Solitaire's analysis of the read out. "There's a couple of scenarios where I could easily get them caught and not have to stop. Just have to find some authority figures at the right spot to do so."

Both vehicles dodging in and out of traffic made the sedan's passenger more cautious as to when he attempted firing, but the occasional gunshot hitting their car could still be heard.

"I know you're scanning for police radio frequencies, but what's your range?" wondered Fredrick.

"Classified, but don't worry. This car's been customized, so my equipment is far more capable than anything commercially available," she replied, keeping her eyes on the road while continuing to switch lanes as necessary.

"Who did the work? The CIA? MI-6 or—"

"Don't go mixing fact and fiction," Solitaire cautioned.

They were approaching another intersection and this time Solitaire got in the far-right hand lane to signal an impending turn.

There had been no gun fire in the last minute or so. The unspoken assumption was either the weapon had to be reloaded, or the shooter was waiting for a better opportunity.

As the light changed, both vehicles started to turn. Unlike Bulevar Kukul-can, this was only a traditional two-lane road so it was totally blocked when the sedan suddenly made a partial U-turn and stopped.

Unfortunately, the micro compact kept going on its new course.

"They were hoping to cut us off, but I never repeat the same maneuver twice," said Solitaire as Fredrick stared at the monitor.

Before the sedan could change course and resume the chase, it was rear ended by a large delivery truck that couldn't stop in time.

The kidnapper's vehicle spun from the force of impact and stopped on the other lane's shoulder.

The closest cars using that lane barely managed to avoid a collision.

The truck driver, after pulling over to his side of the road, got out and ran to check on the sedan's occupants as the flashing roof lights of a police car approached the scene.

"I don't think we'll have any more problems on our journey today," Solitaire announced.

After several side roads, they were back on the boulevard when Fredrick announced, "The Canadian Consulate is up ahead."

A Spanish language road sign on the right indicated the exit for the building was a kilometer away.

"Good. The only problem reaching its American counterpart now will be having to make a left past the Consulate and doubling back to it."

"Somehow I don't think that's going to be a problem for you, fair Juliet," Fredrick replied, taking a longer look at his rescuer than she preferred.

Solitaire just smiled and kept driving.

CHAPTER 9

After everything they had been through, their objective was finally in sight. Yet Fredrick Andrews was surprised when the woman he knew only as 'Juliet' pulled into the parking lot of an adjacent building instead of the United States Consulate property. The car was left idling in a space facing their destination as she reached behind the driver's seat for the tote bag that was part of her current disguise.

"What's wrong?" he asked, looking around but not seeing anything amiss.

"Nothing, I hope," Solitaire replied, while pulling out a pair of binoculars. "Yet it's better to use an ounce of prevention than a pound of cure," she added, while studying what lied ahead. "Can you please push the last button on the far right under the monitor?"

Andrews complied. While the screen display never changed from what the rear-view camera was seeing, an audio transmission now played over the car's stereo system.

"Hmm…" she said, listening to the Spanish broadcast. "The police are looking for a pequeño coche azul."

"A small blue car," translated Andrews.

"Si, with a male and female inside as 'people of interest' in a recent traffic incident," said Solitaire. "Not that I plan to take any chances, but thankfully they don't seem to have any pertinent details, like our plate number. Guess our traveling companions didn't get a good look at me back at the hotel." *Not that it matters, because this disguise will only be active for another hour or so at most.*

"That and they probably didn't want to admit a woman driver outsmarted them," Fredrick said with a smile.

Solitaire just nodded before adding, "Provided they don't catch us before I drop you off, we're free and clear as far as the law is concerned."

"Because then there will only be a woman driving and that will throw everyone off," realized Andrews. "I noticed they didn't say anything about arresting the guys chasing us," he observed, not commenting about his rescuer being able to eavesdrop on police frequencies as well as track patrol cars.

"No, but we might have missed that part," she conceded as they continued listening, although the announcements had switched to other matters for the moment. "What I'm more worried about is that either of those two in the car or any of our playmates back at the hotel, provided they woke up in time to do so before security found them, could have called in reinforcements to head us off at the pass, so to speak. Do you recognize anyone or anything over there?" Solitaire asked, while handing him the binoculars.

Fredrick was a bit taken aback at first how powerful the instrument was, for everything looked like it was practically right in front of him instead of many yards away. He studied the Consulate facade, which looked like any other basic four-story office building. There was a hint of someone—hopefully a security guard—standing inside by the glass partitions of the main entrance. Of more concern were the cars still in the parking lot. Whether those belonged to employees, visitors, or someone potentially lying in wait was unknown.

"No, but I am comprehending your point now," he replied. "Yet would they dare attempt ambushing us on United States property and risk starting an international incident?"

"Depends upon how badly they want us. Or at least you," she replied, taking the binoculars back from him to store away. "Despite the long-term misconception, American foreign service posts are technically not United States property under the Fourteenth Amendment to the Constitution. Only official Embassies are. However, you'll be safe once you're actually in the building. They could still try to make some kind of a last ditch effort against us, but I have a plan," announced Solitaire, before explaining what Andrews needed to do and when while stashing the tote bag back behind the driver's seat, but in such a way that it could be grabbed quickly again when needed.

Fredrick contemplated her plan and asked, "Once I'm inside, then what happens?"

"Although I'd appreciate leaving me out of it as much as possible, after you tell them everything you've been through over the last couple of days, they'll start a formal investigation in cooperation with the local authorities. Granted, I don't know how much that will actually achieve," admitted Solitaire, "but at least in time the Consulate can oversee getting you back to the states and home safely."

"And then this nightmare will be over?"

"At least your part of it. Just stay close to home for awhile until my team and I get this matter fully resolved," she advised, while turning off the radio.

He gave her a puzzled look.

"What? I'm just taking point here in Cancun. You didn't think I'm working alone, did you?"

"The thought never crossed my mind until just now."

"I appreciate your concern, but I knew the job would be dangerous when I took it. Yet even with you safely back home, someone still has a major grudge against your father and that needs to be addressed," Solitaire reminded him. *Maybe your business and even the rest of your family as well,* was her silent addition.

"Yeah. I've been thinking about that between gunfire and other hazards but unfortunately, I'm still drawing a blank on who it might be, let alone why."

Then Fredrick paused, silently staring at her before inquiring, "Are you going to be okay?"

"No reason why I shouldn't be," she calmly replied.

"I… I just want to say thank you while I still have the chance. If we ever meet again, I hope it's under better circumstances but whoever you're married to better realize just how lucky they are."

"I think they do," Solitaire solemnly replied, thinking of all the good anonymously accomplished so far in her time as the latest in a long line of Secret Samaritans.

There was an awkward silence between them before she turned to face what lied ahead and said, "Let's get you home."

+++

The pequeño coche azul slowly left the parking lot, traveling right at the speed limit to complete the short trip to their destination.

But once the blue micro compact started to pull onto the Consulate property, Solitaire gunned the engine and made a bee line straight for the front entrance.

Upon spotting the new arrival, two men got out of a parked car. Any view of the rifles they carried were currently blocked by the vehicle doors as their target jumped the outer curb at a high rate of speed.

Yet as they brought their weapons to bear, one man had a brief moment of hesitation. "I know we're to kill the driver and take the guy alive, but if a stray shot should happen to hit the Consulate or someone unlucky to be in the wrong place at the wrong time…"

The rear tires ascended the curb as Solitaire's car drove onto the bordering sidewalk, passenger side facing the building.

"I know," said his partner, lowering his rifle. "We can always get the gringo at the airport more quietly later. Let's follow her and have some fun."

"Si," the driver agreed as they both got back into their car, thankful that the azul auto's noisy arrival kept anyone from noticing them or the weapons.

+++

Not knowing what was going on, the Security Guard inside by the front entrance drew his weapon and called for reinforcement on his radio as the blue intruder approached his position.

The compact pulled even with the entrance. Fredrick Andrews lowered the passenger window and crawled out because there wasn't enough space between car and building to open the door.

Squatting between vehicle and Consulate, he started banging on the glass door. "Please let me in! I'm an American!"

"We close to the public at 1:30 weekdays, local time," announced the guard. "These doors only open by appointment between now and 8:30 tomorrow morning. Can you prove—"

"My name is Fredrick Andrews," the man on the ground said, holding up his Identification. "For the last few days I've been held against my will in Suite 810 of the Hotel Paradiso."

"We got a missing person's notice on a Fredrick Andrews yesterday," a voice behind the Security Guard said as more personnel arrived.

With that the guard opened the door and let Andrews crawl inside before locking it behind him again.

The moment Fredrick was safely within, Solitaire drove away.

Yet she didn't leave the Consulate property alone.

CHAPTER 10

The micro compact headed down Bulevar Kukulcan back toward the Canadian Consulate.

When she stopped at the next light, Solitaire reached behind and moved her tote bag onto the empty passenger seat.

Despite what I told Andrews, I'll need a different disguise for the return flight to the States to insure whoever is behind this mess doesn't make another attempt on him. Even though traveling under the other gender has become more difficult in recent years it will have to be male this time, since I'm supposed to be part of a recovery team. Thankfully I planted enough false clues in our conversation that even if Fredrick attempts to find out who I am, he'll be on the wrong path.

As the light changed and she started forward, Solitaire smiled at the monitor display.

Two more men in a green car this time, huh? Guess I was right about their employer having some deep pockets, she surmised. *Hope you have the guts to chase a lioness Señors.*

With that she pushed her foot down upon the gas pedal.

+++

"She spotted us," the passenger complained as the blue car pulled further away from them.

"So? That just makes it even more fun when we catch her," the driver replied with a smile as he increased speed too.

Both men had stowed their rifles on the back seat under a tarp before leaving the American Consulate. Unaware of the target's bulletproofing, the passenger traveled with a handgun in his lap. Yet between the heavy traffic and wanting to question the driver before killing her, he just stared at the car's rear hatch and contemplated the future.

They traveled for kilometers down the road. Green keeping pace with blue, who always maintained a slight lead.

However, both men were briefly caught off guard when the compact suddenly made a right turn into a large shopping center without signaling.

The sedan's driver-side wheels jumped the median separating traffic going in and out of the retail complex they now entered. Its operator cursed at the impact while his passenger was thankful he had his weapon's safety on.

The two men watched with some confusion as their target turned left and pulled into a remote section of the parking lot far from any store. There it came to a full stop with the automobile straddling adjoining empty spaces.

"Is she surrendering?" the driver wondered aloud.

"Doesn't matter to me," his partner replied with an evil grin on his face.

The hunters drew closer until their car's front bumper almost touched their prey's rear.

Yet before either man could get out of their vehicle, ominous black smoke poured out of the other car's tailpipes.

"Maldita sea!" cursed the driver. "I can't see a thing!"

"She must have engine trouble. We've got her!" the passenger exclaimed. He happily stepped out with gun drawn but stopped and tried to cover his face. "Dios! The hedor!" he cried.

"Ser valiente," replied the driver, as he pulled a handgun from his shoulder holster. Now outside the car, he would never admit his partner was right about the stench.

Although no one but them were in this remote section, both men hoped the smoke would hide their weapons from public view.

Their eyes started to water from the strong smell. Neither man could see very well through the thick haze, so extended their free arms to feel their way toward the compact.

There was no chance to comment on the fact that the target now seemed farther away than it should be. There was also no opportunity to react to the danger they faced as the smoke changed color from black to green.

Within moments both men passed out. Their unconscious bodies fell mercilessly to the hard pavement beneath them as the micro compact drove away.

Glad that stunt worked, thought Solitaire, observing events the best she could via the thermal imaging option of the rear-view camera. *Even though I just let the car slowly pull itself forward a couple of feet, I couldn't risk going too far and have the knockout gas lose its effectiveness dispersing in the open air. Now to find some place secure to pull my next trick.*

+++

The blue car drove away from the scene with no indication of anything coming from its tailpipes. When and by who the unconscious gunmen would be found was out of Solitaire's hands as she approached the shopping complex.

She took note of the retailers either already closed for the day or that soon would be as Cancun prepared for another robust night of revelry.

Driving to the complex's end, the car turned at the corner business' rear and idled behind the building near its loading dock.

There a rather androgynous looking American tourist with black hair and no tan to speak of got out of the car, leaving the driver's side door open in the process. Solitaire had slipped off the sundress to reveal the beach shorts underneath before hastily donning a t-shirt and wig from the tote bag while executing the smoke trick.

A quick look at the micro compact revealed a few spots on the body that might need to be buffed out where the shots fired at it struck. Like drifting clouds in the sky, there were now small hints of white within the otherwise solid blue color. Without a second thought, Solitaire reached out and started peeling away the car's outer coating as if it was dead skin from a sunburn.

This special polymeric vinyl Daye Industries developed sure has its uses, thought Solitaire, as the last of the blue was quickly stripped away and tossed inside a trash bag behind the driver's seat.

As the Covert Crusader got back behind the wheel of the now totally white car, another dashboard button rotated the license plates to a different set than what was displayed.

The auto body's physical scars could still be seen upon close inspection, but anyone looking for a woman driving a blue micro compact would not find her or it now as Solitaire left the shopping complex and started a roundabout route back to the local sanctuary.

+++

Within two hours of careful driving to make sure she was neither being tailed nor at risk of being pulled over by the local authorities and have them accidentally stumble upon something they shouldn't, Solitaire reached her destination. After stowing her equipment and taking a long hot shower, she got dressed then contacted a special, very private website to file a maintenance request.

Don't know how the Daye Foundation handles repairs and upkeep whenever the Solitaire on duty isn't around, but the car should have a new paint job and plates too for whatever its next mission might be. After all, I'm not the only one with secrets to protect.

Once everything was taken care of, the woman pretending to be Frieda Daye covertly left the hidden hideout. Walking a few blocks to a more public location, she used her cellphone to summon a taxi for the return trip to the family villa.

+++

"Señorita Frieda, welcome home," Fernando said warmly as he opened the door for the mistress of the hacienda.

"It is good to be home," the tired lady said, while brushing aside a stray strand of blonde wig hair. "I'm sorry I didn't call Ramone for a ride back, but I had no idea how long I'd be out today." *It was bad enough having him drive me to a legitimate office building as Frieda and then sneaking back to the Cancun safe house as somebody else.*

"I trust things went well for you today?" he asked, staring at her briefcase.

"They did, but—" Then the disguised Solitaire paused as she sniffed the air. "Do I smell—"

"Si. Consuela has been cooking a big feast all day for you and—"

"I'll be right back down to eat after I wash up," promised Solitaire with a smile, rushing upstairs both in character and genuinely looked forward to a home cooked meal before breaking the news about having to leave Cancun.

In the bedroom reserved for the real Daye sibling, she tossed her purse and briefcase on the bed before going into the adjoining bathroom.

A couple of minutes later Solitaire came back into the main room, only to see a gun pointed directly at her!

CHAPTER 11

Whether due to exhaustion after a long mission or the assumption of being within a safe environment, Solitaire silently chastised herself for letting someone get the drop on her.

The new arrival stood in front of the now closed bedroom door.

The two women stared intently at each other. Solitaire instantly recognized her potential assailant and could tell by the way she held the Italian Beretta pointed directly at her chest that the slightly gray-haired lady meant business.

While several possibilities instantly came to mind, there was too much open space between them. At least one shot would be fired before any disarming tactic could be executed.

"Who are you and why are you impersonating my daughter?" the other woman demanded to know.

"I meant no harm or disrespect," Solitaire began, "but pretending to be Frieda was my quickest viable access to Cancun and if Frieda stayed anywhere else it would look suspicious. I was told that if I ever meet any member of the Daye family to introduce myself as Roseilita."

The other lady's eyes grew wide upon recognizing both the name and the anagram within it. "You're the Foundation's latest Solitaire?"

"Yes."

"Well," the woman said, lowering the gun now in her left hand after making sure the safety was on. "I admit to being a bit taken aback when Fernando informed me Frieda was here after she told me just this morning that business in Madrid would keep her busy there for at least a couple of more days." Moving closer and extending her now empty right hand, she added, "We haven't been formally introduced. I'm—"

"Agatha Clemens Daye, current Matriarch of the Daye Family," Solitaire said, acknowledging she knew the other woman's identity as they shook hands.

"I hate that word. Makes me sound older than I actually am," complained Agatha, while brushing back a strand of gray in her right temple. "Though technically I'm co-Matriarch," she added, while moving to the desk. "My fraternal twin Claudia was born about seven minutes before me. She's the Solitaire program's actual overseer at the moment but brought me in to help manage expenditures and logistics."

Sitting in the desk chair and laying the gun atop its surface, Agatha wondered, "What brings you to Cancun?"

"Business," Solitaire replied as she moved to sit on the corner edge of the

"Who are you and why are you impersonating my daughter?"

bed. Now facing her hostess, she explained about Reginald and Fredrick Andrews.

"While I can't recall any of the Daye subsidiaries having had much business dealing with them, Andrews is a big name in aviation. Any idea what's behind it all?" Agatha asked after Solitaire finished.

A shoulder shrug heralded "Corporate greed? Personal vendetta? Someone definitely has an agenda against at least Reginald, if not the rest of his family too, but at the moment I'm afraid your guess is as good as mine," admitted the Secret Samaritan. "I do need to make arrangements to follow Fredrick back to the states both to continue this assignment and make sure whoever is behind it all doesn't try either another kidnapping or something worse."

"Assuming he'll be safe back home until you've resolved this," Agatha observed. "Well, knowing the American State Department like I do, even if they expedite the matter, the earliest they'll have Andrews mobile will be sometime tomorrow afternoon. That leaves you plenty of time to prepare and for us to get acquainted."

"Oh?" Solitaire asked with some confusion.

"While the Daye Foundation—just a small part of the overall family holdings—secretly funds and operates the Solitaire program, very few of us have any real knowledge of its workings, let alone the personnel involved. For plausible deniability, as they say," Agatha revealed. "You're the first agent I've actually met. I've so many questions."

"I see," Solitaire said with a smile. "I'll answer what I can. Confidentiality and all that."

"Of course," agreed Agatha. "I'm sorry to keep staring at you, but your current resemblance to my daughter is uncanny. I know agents are trained in the art of disguise, but—"

"It's easier to create a whole new identity, compared to impersonating someone specific," conceded Solitaire. "In this case Frieda was physically the easiest Daye for me to be. Her voice is just a tad higher than my normal tone. We're the same height, but there's a bit of theatrical padding between my cheeks and teeth to accurately portray her facial structure and much more within my brassiere to approximate Frieda's bust size, along with the right wig and color contact lenses."

"Like I said, if it wasn't for talking to her this morning, the only thing that might give you away is your hair's parted the wrong way," revealed Agatha.

"It is?" the impostor said, reaching up to check the strands.

"Frieda parts hers toward the right, while yours is leaning toward the left."

"It's how the best photograph I had of her to base my disguise on showed it."

"Then the image must have gotten flipped somehow. It wouldn't matter to anyone who hasn't seen her in a while, like the household staff here. But still…"

"Good to know. I'll be more careful in the future," promised Solitaire, *especially since I'm still wondering about the Reginald Andrews mustache situation.* "Now then, I have a question. How did this all start? My trainers either couldn't or wouldn't tell me, and my predecessor admitted she didn't know before we parted company and I took over full time."

Agatha was about to answer when there was a knock on the door. "¿Señora Agatha? ¿Señorita Frieda?" called out Fernando.

"¿Si?" said Agatha.

"Will you be dining downstairs or should I bring trays to you?" he asked in English

"We'll be down soon. Just got wrapped up talking family business," answered Agatha.

"Bueno," said Fernando in the hallway.

The ladies remained silent until the sound of receding footsteps faded. Then Solitaire asked, "He didn't hear…"

"I'll check," said Agatha, while pulling out her cellphone from a pocket of the dark slacks she had on. "He went back downstairs after talking to us and…" A few screen swipes and pushed icons revealed "No. According to the security monitor timestamp, he came to the door just as you were finishing that comment about taking over," while holding the phone up so her guest could see the footage replay itself on the screen. "Even if he heard that, Fernando wouldn't know the context.

"Now then, I'll have to pop back to my room long enough to secure this," Agatha said, grabbing the gun with her free hand after standing. "Consuela is a great cook and has been working in the kitchen like mad ever since I arrived this morning. Shall we dine?"

CHAPTER 12

From her position beside the base of the portable reviewing stand at Joint Base Andrews in Prince George's County, Maryland, the excited executive looked up at the assembled throng. Not only were the three tiers of seats completely full with representatives from every branch of America's armed forces, there was no one less than a decorated Colonel present if you ignored their aides and assorted guards. *Okay Ariel, calm down,* she told herself while anxiously fingering the amethyst pendant on the gold chain around her neck. *After they see the prototype in action, the orders will start pouring in,* was her happy thought.

Carol Evans stood nearby while checking her watch. "Almost time Ariel," she said loud enough for only her superior to hear.

With a head nod to acknowledge the assistant that caused her matching amethyst earrings to briefly dangle, Ariel Andrews turned to face those behind them and asked, "Are you ready?"

Two technicians in matching company jumpsuits sat at a folding table, each monitoring what was about to happen via computer tablets. After a brief glance at his companion who nodded affirmatively, the man closest to his employer just smiled and made a 'thumbs up' gesture with one hand.

Ariel glanced down and double checked her appearance, brushing a stray piece of lint off the otherwise pristine formal but feminine styled white business suit with her free hand. The other held a wireless microphone, perhaps a bit tighter than necessary.

"Then let's do this," the lady said, before walking around to the front of the crowd. She stopped and stood facing them next to another folding table. While much smaller than the one the technicians sat at, it was no less important, as indicated by the private security guard on either end and whatever sat upon it being covered by a royal purple sateen cloth that almost matched the color of her jewelry stones.

She smiled while activating the microphone, then began to speak.

"Hello and thank you all for coming. The equipment needs of the United States' military forces have grown dramatically since that fateful night General Washington led his troops across the Delaware. Especially the last couple of decades with technology improving on practically a daily basis. That is why I'm here today to present and demonstrate Andrews Aviation's new XDS Reconnaissance Drone," Ariel announced, as the security guards removed the cloth to reveal the prototype.

"As you can see, our latest creation is no larger than previous models and despite the basic gray for today's demonstration, is available in all the standard public flight and camouflage color schemes."

Even with a rotor blade at each corner for lift and mobility, the drone's outer dimensional perimeter measured less than the average size loaf of bread.

"As promised in the initial proposal submitted earlier this year for review, using new construction materials, we have decreased its overall weight by ten percent without compromising any of the previous model's capabilities." The executive quietly noticed some of the audience sitting up a bit straighter at that revelation before adding, "In fact we've also been able to include a new atmospheric odor analyzer, or smell sensor if you prefer, to our recon drone. The XDS can accurately detect more traditional elements like smoke if there's a fire nearby, along with drug making ingredients and other chemicals, like those used in manufacturing bombs. Hence the initials for Extreme Drug Sniffer."

That certainly got everyone's attention, thought Ariel, noticing all eyes were now fully upon her and the prototype.

"But as they say, actions speak louder than words. Gentlemen."

With that cue, a button was pushed on a digital keyboard to activate the machine.

The rotors spun in unison as the unit lifted sightly off its display stand. Ariel briefly held her microphone over the hovering drone before pointing out to the audience, "The XDS-1 is even quieter than its predecessor, with no exterior noise to be heard until the mic is practically in direct contact with it."

With a brief glance at the technicians, the drone was sent higher up.

At first it just hovered over the display table. Then the device moved from side to side before briefly going forward and backwards, never moving far away from its starting point as Andrews talked about its maneuverability after vertical takeoff.

"Now for the piece de resistance. As you can see, out in the field behind me are three average size shipping crates. Each has an assortment of packing peanuts, ground coffee and other assorted stuff typically used by smugglers to mask the scent of any illegal contraband. Yet, while his men were setting up our testing range, General Wayne had one of them hide a container holding less than a quarter ounce of Nitrocellulose at my request. Only the General and his man know in which," revealed Ariel.

Those closest to him turned to look at the officer, who simply nodded in confirmation of what was said.

"Nitrocellulose is a harmless ingredient of some paint lacquers and printing inks, but is more deadly within rocket propellants and explosives. While it will naturally be up to the drone operators and those above them to determine what actions—if any—are taken afterwards, the XDS-1 is now going to find our hidden chemical."

As Ariel finished speaking, the technicians initiated the search protocol.

Leaving its position over the display table, the drone flew in a straight line directly toward the center of the field, where the three crates were placed about ten yards apart from each other.

Everyone but Carol Evans expected it to stop and hover over the central container before examining the trio and report which one held the hidden chemical.

Instead, the XDS-1 flew past the crates and kept going!

"What—" Ariel said in shock, barely keeping her composure in front of the assembled officers. She calmly walked over to the technicians with the microphone off, who responded before she could speak.

"It's got to be an unforeseen glitch," the one who gave her the thumbs up gesture said. "Maybe it picked up a stronger scent?"

"Yet it's not reporting anything except the Nitrocellulose was in the crate on the far left," countered the second technician, while nervously fidgeting in her seat.

"Recall—"

"We've been trying, but the XDS-1 isn't responding," replied the first, double checking the monitor readout.

"Why?" Ariel demanded to know.

"Unknown at this time," was all either employee could say.

"Tracking?" Ariel asked.

"It's continuing northward, about to leave Andrews property and—" the man hastily pushed some buttons before adding, "Its transponder went offline just as it crossed the border into public land!"

"Send the search team out to find it. Then secure everything and get ready to leave. Not a word to anyone, even among yourselves, until we get back to the hangar," Ariel ordered, before returning to face the crowd.

"Well folks, I'm afraid I've got some good news and bad news," the executive began when the mic was back on. "The XDS-1 has gone after a much stronger scent than our test subject, so we'll have to reschedule the rest of the demonstration at everyone's convenience on a later date, after we've had a chance to examine today's results and correct this issue."

With that everyone started to rise.

"But before you leave, a quick question for General Wayne."

An older man in the middle of the second row stopped and looked at the executive.

"Was the Nitrocellulose in the crate on the far left?" Ariel asked.

His face showed genuine surprise before replying, "Yes, it was."

As a round of applause began, Ariel Andrews smiled and took a slight bow, but her thoughts were much darker. *I've at least managed to save some face today but now I've got to get the XDS-1 back, figure out who's trying to ruin my company and stop them before it's too late!*

+++

A few miles north of the combined Naval Air and Military Air Force base, a casually dressed Hispanic male stood in the center of a local park with a pair of binoculars, but it was not birds he scanned the sky for.

Upon spotting a gray flying object, Damián Garcia turned and started walking back toward a nondescript panel van parked at the curb beyond the sidewalk encircling the park.

From the front passenger seat, César Fernandez watched a trusted member of his Anbessas gang approach as someone within opened the van's sliding door.

"Any moment now," Garcia announced, entering the vehicle.

"Confirmed," Alberto Aguilar said from inside the cargo area while intently watching his laptop computer screen.

They were a team of four. Each had taken turns driving with someone in the front passenger seat and the other two in back since leaving Miami the day before. Those not on duty rested in sleeping bags the best they could. Besides regular stops to purchase food and fuel to go, along with necessary restroom breaks, the only other pause in their journey was to find a discrete location to change license plates once along the way. A similar stop would be made on the return trip to replace the van's legitimate Florida plates before ditching the set stolen in South Carolina.

All eyes turned to watch through either the open side door or front passenger window as the XDS-1 lowered its altitude. Once at the proper height, it entered the van and landed on the bare metal floor.

The man who opened the door for the alleged birdwatcher hastily shut it again as Alberto announced, "We've got it boss! Your inside guy really came through. Especially with the info to update this laptop for the job."

"Good," replied César. Having never bothered to tell those under him who the inside 'guy' was, he turned to address the others more properly as the fourth man made his way back to the driver's seat. "That little thing is not only going to make us rich beyond your wildest dreams, but it's just the start of what the Anbessas can accomplish." *Including my revenge against Reginald Andrews.*

"And it's not even eight thirty yet," César added while glancing at his watch. "Let's head home and celebrate our victory. Besides, I'm surely not the only one looking forward to sleeping on something softer than this van's floor tonight."

CHAPTER 13

A disguised Solitaire had maintained a lone, old fashioned surveillance vigil of the American Consulate since noon. Even if she knew whether they would book Fredrick Andrews' ticket home in advance or wait until the last possible moment to do so, it was too dangerous to attempt digitally sneaking into their computer for she did not want to be caught within a foreign country trying to hack another government's system. Besides the risk of exposing herself, the Solitaire program and the Daye Foundation; capture would result in major charges, including espionage and possibly terrorism too.

Instead, before the false Frieda left the Daye hacienda for 'family business' elsewhere, she set up a passive software program that discretely monitored the passenger lists for all flights back to Florida, especially those flying directly to Miami. Her disposable cellphone would ping upon each new reservation booked while she sat in disguise behind the steering wheel of another car from the Cancun sanctuary. Between her parking space at a busy nearby retail outlet and a very good pair of binoculars, covertly observing the Consulate building was relatively easy but tedious.

During their dinner Agatha Daye offered to help, but Solitaire couldn't guarantee her safety since there was no way of knowing how whoever was behind recent events might try to strike at Fredrick again if that was still on their agenda.

If others were about during dinner, the two talked as mother and daughter but, when possible, the conversation was more akin to two newfound friends being open and honest with each other.

"So how many current members of the Daye family know about me and my job?" Solitaire wondered at one point, after Fernando had removed their empty plates to bring in the next course.

"The oldest Daye of each generation is charged with making sure the operation continues. When the time comes, either Claudia or I will have to inform the next in line, who will be trained to assume overseeing the program when we're no longer able to, but that is it at the moment. The rest of the family are only told when they're old enough to understand to trust Roseilita with no last name if they should ever meet her or ask for her through the website if they need help," Agatha revealed.

"Because if a last name's given, it's an impostor."

"Right. Otherwise, except for a few key employees at the center of it all, the rest of those in service to the Solitaire program think they're just going about regular Daye Industries duties and assignments whenever a task arises. But doesn't it get to you at times?" Agatha asked.

"Does what?"

"The loneliness. Being out there alone, facing whatever you have to?"

"Well, the name and nature of the program are in regard to a lone operative, not a team. Besides, all those psych evaluations proved I can handle the job."

"Along with all the other requirements to even be considered for training, let alone actually become a field agent," Agatha added.

The recollection was interrupted by another ping from her phone. One that Solitaire had mixed feelings about.

Dang! While they should be leaving for the airport in another hour or so, Andrews is booked for passage home under his own name. Does this mean the Consulate thinks the threat is over or are they using him as bait to flush out whoever they can catch? Either way, this won't make my job any easier, she realized before going online to book her own ticket for that same flight. Afterward, Solitaire ended the program remotely and cleared all the airport data from the phone except for her reservation. Although the battery was reading 98%, it would stay on the car charger until she reached her destination.

+++

Having been to both, the only difference Solitaire personally saw between the Cancun International Airport and its Cozumel counterpart was location. The former being located further up the Mexican Coast, flights could cross the Gulf of Mexico to the United States quicker than any from the latter.

With the binoculars back in their case under the front passenger seat, her vehicle safely trailed a few car lengths behind the Consulate sedan. Close enough to keep them in sight and take action if necessary, but far enough away to not be considered a potential threat.

At least they're taking security somewhat seriously, she thought, having seen Fredrick placed in the back seat between two men while the driver and another man rode in the front. The Consulate trio looked like typical transferred Americans to her. Men who's skin was a little darker than normal only because they went to the beach as often as their schedules allowed.

Solitaire wasn't happy that they traveled a direct route to the airport. The other driver never made a sudden turn nor took any other evasive maneuvers to make sure they weren't being followed. *I'm still uncertain how or if another attempt will be made, but I hope their auto is bulletproof.*

Upon reaching their destination without incident, Solitaire had to take the risk of detouring to leave her two-door coupe in a long term parking area. After finding a discrete space, the alarm code was set and the door locked. She sent a brief text with its location to a private e-address. Whoever came from the collection service to take the car back and prepare it for the next time either she or a future Solitaire agent might be in Cancun would find the keys and garage stub within the glove compartment and pay the fee on their way out.

Unable to wait for a shuttle bus, an average looking business man in a light blue leisure suit with only a carryon bag flung over one shoulder, started making his way from the garage toward the terminal. If anyone noticed his fast pace, they simply assumed he was trying to catch his flight.

In part this was true. Once inside, a quick look at the Departures Schedule posted along one wall confirmed the information Solitaire had. Yet even with knowing which flight, its gate and estimated takeoff time, she wanted to get Fredrick Andrews back under observation as quickly as possible.

Electronically checking in was relatively quick but going through both airport security and International Customs since American tourist Alistair Burke was leaving the country to return home, turned out to be more time consuming. *Which is why they're always urging travelers to leave extra early nowadays,* mused the disguised Secret Samaritan as she put Burke's shoes back on.

With so much scrutiny on an international flight, the cosmetics were minimal. Her natural short hair was completely dyed to the scalp a different color with just contact lenses—Burke needed corrective lens for proper vision, without any mention of them altering eye hue—and very carefully applied false fingerprint applications to match records implanted in American data bases long ago. Special equipment was kept to a bare minimum too, but hopefully enough was available if needed.

Her biggest hurdle was being a woman dressed as a man. While most travel disguises were under Solitaire's own gender whenever possible, not every situation allowed for that convenience. The biometric readings of airport scanning equipment were much more sophisticated today and could easily detect the physical differences between genders hidden by clothing.

Thankfully some countries were now more understanding than they used to be. As long as the correct box on the passport was marked in regards to Gender Identification, Alistair Burke could legally go wherever they wanted to.

Cleared by security, Solitaire stepped into the main waiting area, noting how airports seemed more akin to miniature cities with their own tourist attractions nowadays.

The terminal's circular interior made it easy for travelers to take in all the shops, food offerings and other attractions from practically any vantage point. The new arrival was no less guilty of people watching than anyone else, but Solitaire searched for one specific person.

She finally spotted Fredrick Andrews standing in the designated waiting area for their flight, but—*He's down to just two escorts. The driver must still be with the car someplace, but where is the third man?*

Solitaire discretely kept an eye on her targets from a distance while pretending to contemplate a window display of summer tourist attire available from a terminal shop as the three men conferred about something. She noted they managed to acquire Andrews some fresh clothing instead of that makeshift outfit he wore leaving the hotel yesterday, but *Their tailor has no imagination whatsoever. They all look like they got their outfits from the same Federal Employees discount store,* she mused, noting each wore a matching dark blue suit.

Then Fredrick and one of his escorts started walking away from the other man. She quickly realized their goal and switched to double checking the flight itinerary board as they went past her without a second thought towards the nearby men's room.

Well, in for a penny... Solitaire figured as she turned to follow but was suddenly blocked from entering by a taller and more muscular man in a black suit.

"I'm sorry Señor. This facility is closed. The next one is to your right five gates down," the living obstacle said. Other than briefly pointing in the general direction away from the restroom, he remained standing in place, confident that this tourist wasn't getting past him.

Definitely local, Solitaire instantly realized, noting a more natural skin tone native to someone of either Hispanic or Caribbean descent who spoke English with a matching accent, *but I see no sign of any type of communications device on him. Is he Airport Security or something else? The wrong move could get me in big trouble.*

Using one of the many rehearsed male voices she could perform, Solitaire's response was, "S-stomach, q-queasy," while Alistair Burke clutched his abdominal area with both arms. The carry-on bag's shoulder strap moved a little, but stayed relatively in place on his right.

Yet what the man blocking the entryway didn't see was Solitaire touching the fake gem on top of an alleged graduating class ring while distracting him with conversation.

"You've got to go to the other restroom," was the man's cold reply.

The disguised Clandestine Crusader took an unsteady step forward while faking a belch far worse sounding than it actually was.

Afraid the stranger in front of him might really be getting sick, the man in Solitaire's way involuntarily took a step back further into the restroom foyer because the last thing he wanted was to be puked on.

Solitaire leaned forward as if she really was about to heave. Her opponent now found himself fully upon the tiled curved path away from the entrance that led into the facility. There was only one course of action to avoid a messy outcome, yet he had his orders that nobody was allowed inside the restroom right now.

No public modern facility possesses a direct entry into its main chamber. Most have either a secondary entrance or some kind of curving path to block the view of passersby before patrons actually reach what they seek.

Now that they were out of probable surveillance camera range, the disguised Solitaire chose that moment to act. Still clutching his stomach,

Alistair Burke moaned and slumped against the wall to his left.

"Let's get you some help," the other man said, moving to usher the tourist out of the restroom. Left unspoken was that outside, the intruder would become someone else's problem.

Yet the moment the man was within range, Solitaire swiftly raised her left hand and pressed the ring against the right side of the man's neck. This allowed the little protrusion that emerged upon touching the ersatz gem to inject a powerful sedative.

Although the attack was physically no worse than a minor mosquito bite, her opponent growled in anger at being duped as the chemical took effect, for Solitaire's aim was true with the shot injected directly into the carotid artery.

Her opponent tried to stay standing and conscious while attempting to grab the man in front of him but lost both battles.

Solitaire easily sidestepped the unsuccessful capture as her opponent's quickly weakening legs gave out on him and he collapsed, deeply asleep by the time he hit the floor.

With a now relatively clear path, it was easy for her to walk over the now unconscious man.

Yet what she found inside the restroom was another matter.

CHAPTER 14

Although worried about Fredrick Andrews, Solitaire knew better than to rush into potential danger.

The trick ring was only good for one use without refilling. Bringing more sedative was among the many things she didn't dare risk trying to sneak through airport security. While there was a small canister of disguised pepper spray available and her shirt buttons could be broken open to expose small doses of the sleeping agent into the air, both would have to be directly in an opponent's face to be most effective.

I'll just have to rely on my wits and fighting skills, she realized.

Cautiously Solitaire walked to the end of the short corridor and stopped right at the edge of the final curve that opened into the men's room proper.

Even crouching to present a lower profile, Solitaire realized she couldn't peer around the corner and risk being spotted by those inside. However, the large rectangular wall mirror, vertically anchored so patrons could double check their appearance before leaving, gave her an idea.

Taking Alistair Burke's sunglasses out of the lone shirt pocket they were in, she aimed the reflective lenses at the mirror. They were just a simple accessory with no ulterior purpose, but their impromptu use gave her a chance to see without being seen.

The glasses had to be angled this way and that to take in the whole restroom. While the reverse image the lenses presented was small, what Solitaire saw surprised her.

Andrews stood behind the Consulate man, who was using plastic zip ties from an unknown source to secure the arms of someone dressed like a janitor. That man was chest down on the tiled floor with a bloody nose. While there was a custodian's cart nearby, the open knife lying on the floor between them and her was more telling.

Was there an assassination attempt against Fredrick? Or did the janitor try kidnapping by force? wondered Solitaire. *Whatever the answer, I can't risk being discovered. Especially not with what's probably an unconscious accomplice nearby.*

Putting the glasses away, Solitaire reached out to the watch on her left wrist. While made to look like a more deluxe model, it was actually just a simple battery-operated time piece with digital display. Holding down the Alarm Setting Button, she turned the upper body of the case counterclockwise to reveal a miniature storage compartment where normally the rest of the circuitry for the fancier version would be in its bottom half.

Carefully taking out one of the two items inside, Solitaire placed the listening device in the grout space between floor tiles and wall as close to the corner as she could unnoticed. Upon the very remote chance anyone actually discovered the device, it resembled a tiny ant, making the greatest danger to the bug either being stepped on or swept away when the floor was cleaned. An acceptable loss since there would be no chance to retrieve it as she turned and quietly left the restroom.

The disguised Discrete Defender sat down and unclipped a cellphone from her pants' belt while passenger Alistair Burke waited for his flight to begin boarding. Yet while the device did have a few songs and a couple of audio books in memory for cover, another use was the hidden app to hear whatever the restroom bug picked up.

So far that consisted of Andrews' long rant of complaints while the Consulate man accomplished nothing trying to question the suspect. *Large room, lousy acoustics considering there's only two active voices,* Solitaire thought, trying to fine tune the reception.

During this time the other Consulate man received a message in his left ear. Although Solitaire could only hear the restroom half of the conversation, that was the man's destination. He was joined at the entrance by the third member of the escort team. *He must have been checking over the plane or something,* Solitaire figured.

They talked in front of the men's room entrance, out of listening device range, before going inside. *One of them can take credit for capturing the accomplice. Unless they know exactly what to look for, the injection point is too small to see with the unaided eye, which is how it got through check in, and any blood test results will be akin to finding a very drunk man, which puts me in the clear.*

Or so she thought.

+++

"Are you okay, sir?" Solitaire overheard someone ask Fredrick before wanting to know what happened.

"Yeah. When we came in this creep was emptying the trash cans but when he saw me, the guy pulled out that knife over there and said I was going with him," Andrews said, answering both questions while probably pointing to the weapon on the floor. "When your man moved to prevent that, the guy tried to kill him. Thankfully your man took care of him like a pro, although I won't deny being scared stiff."

"You're all right. That's the main thing," the same voice told Andrews before asking the other man, "He say anything?"

"Not a word in any language."

"Say Clark, did you have any company other than him?"

"No Hal."

"Hear anything?"

"I was a little busy. Why?" Clark inquired, giving Solitaire some help identifying the two men.

"Barry's securing another suspect we found unconscious on the way in here," Hal replied, identifying their partner in the process.

"Probably to keep anyone out while this guy did his work. Then the two of them would have gotten Andrews out of here somehow," surmised Clark.

"That's what we figured, but Barry saw a guy encounter our other suspect before he lost sight of them starting to enter the restroom. Only the stranger left, so we're trying to figure out what happened."

Damn! I was spotted, cursed Solitaire, *but at best I'm just a maybe to them at the moment.*

"It must have been another member of Juliet's team," guessed Fredrick. "She did say she wasn't working alone."

I asked you not to talk about that, Solitaire silently grumbled.

"Probably," replied Hal. "Yet other than asking about your status, your father wouldn't say anything to us. We need to know who he hired."

"Why should he tell you?" asked Andrews in return. "Client privilege and all that."

"I don't think that applies in this case. Other than maybe against the bad guys, this mysterious team hasn't broken any laws that we're aware of, but we want to make sure that they're officially licensed and authorized to work outside the United States, let alone in Cancun. After all, the last thing we want is an international incident on our hands if they do something they shouldn't," explained Hal.

"You mean like rescuing a kidnapped American being held hostage on foreign soil?" Fredrick replied.

"I'm just saying—"

"Hal, I think we should be tending to our prisoners and making sure Andrews gets safely on his flight," suggested Clark, interrupting the conversation. "The other team is waiting in Miami to make sure he gets home safely."

Hal agreed but announced his intention of identifying and running a background check on the man Barry saw. "Even though we haven't identified this mysterious Juliet by running the hotel's surveillance footage through facial recognition yet."

"We both know that takes time. Especially if we have to expand the search internationally," Clark reminded him. "The size of America's database alone—"

Solitaire put the cellphone away before the group emerged to prevent looking any more suspicious than she might already be before Alistair Burke rose and casually walked over to the nearest kiosk to window shop as if he didn't have a care in the world. It was easy to pretend not noticing the Consulate men coming out of the restroom and look around for their other suspect as Airport Security approached to take custody of the prisoners.

Yet Solitaire's mind raced through possibilities.

Past Solitaires had it a lot easier maintaining aliases before the technology boom at the start of this millennium, but there's several potential ways to overcome this. The main problem is how far they might probe my false background. Any identity I assume can survive an initial computer search but if anyone tries doing a much deeper confirmation inquiry, let alone a physical 'boots on the ground' type investigation to confirm things, the alias won't last long.

Despite needing to do so to a point with any questions concerning the gender issue, no Solitaire had ever fully complied with the regulations from the American Transportation Security Administration and other agencies for travelers to list all current and previous nicknames and aliases on their passports. A requirement which usually just covered the issue of maiden

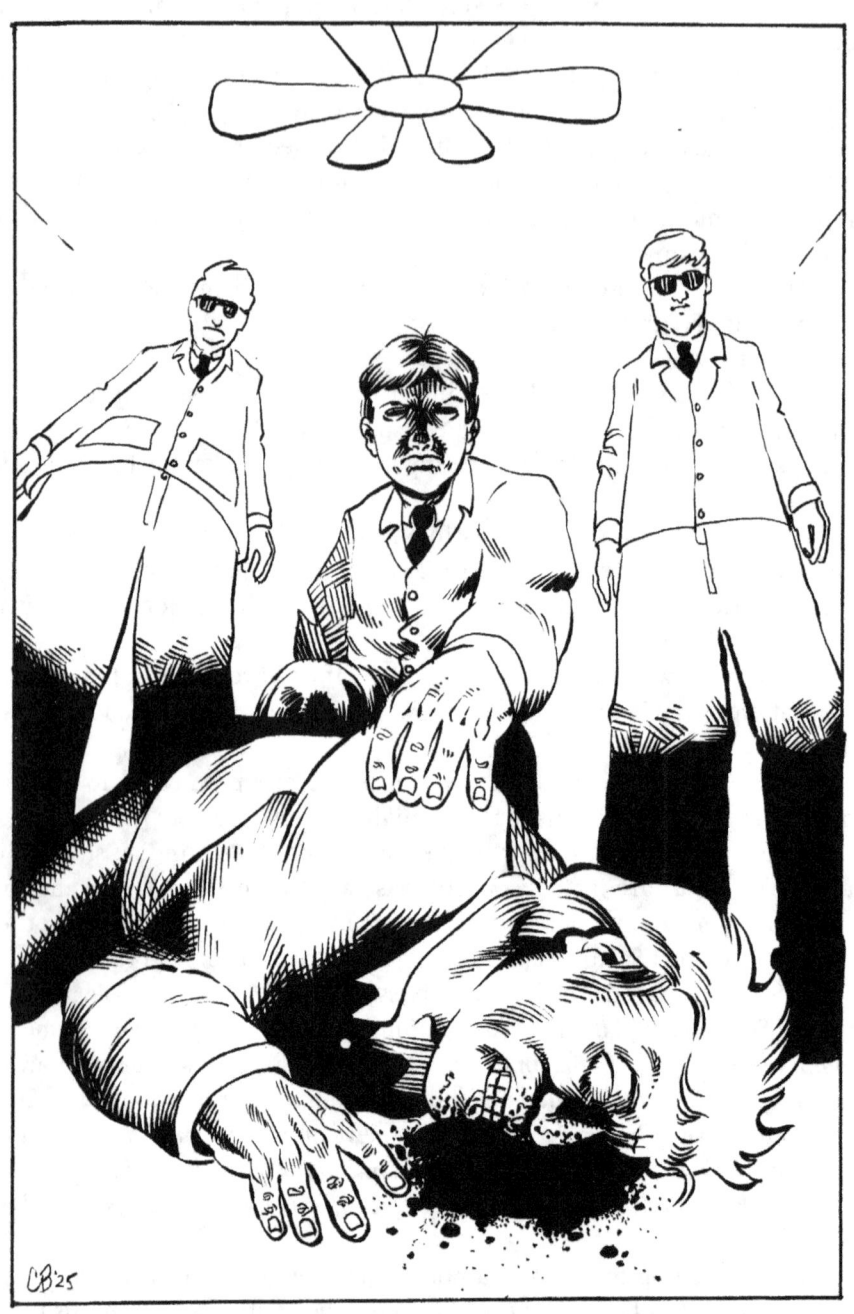

"I think we should be tending to our prisoner."

versus married surnames. *If they can prove Alistair Burke doesn't exist, I'm facing at least temporary detention if not outright arrest while they investigate further. Something I don't dare risk.*

The main difficulty was only Burke could officially go through customs in Miami. Leaving the airport and establishing another identity to fly back to the states was possible but out of the question, for it would require valuable time. Solitaire didn't want to lose track of Andrews if his mystery enemy made another kidnapping attempt.

If I need to get 'lost' once we've landed, I can remove the contact lenses and find someplace to change clothes. The hair dye will wash out with just plain water and the chemical agent posing as my still factory sealed travel size bottle of mouthwash in the toiletries case, since this color needed to last longer than the maid disguise. But while I still have digital access to them, I couldn't bring the credentials of another alias with me without making airport security suspicious.

Solitaire's thoughts were interrupted by the announcement of her flight about to begin boarding procedures.

With that she turned and headed toward the gate.

CHAPTER 15

As Alistair Burke and the others waited their turn, Solitaire saw one of the three American agents accompany Fredrick Andrews among the First Class passengers who boarded the plane. *Full service back to the United States,* she mused. The red-haired Consulate man was at least a head taller and more muscular than either his charge or her. She did find it odd that while knowing Andrews had no luggage, neither did his escort. *Must have been checked in before I first spotted them.*

Upon being allowed on the plane, it was no surprise to see Fredrick by a window while the other man had the aisle seat next to him to minimize target access.

Even if there had been one available when booking hers, it wouldn't look right for Burke to be sitting in First Class too. Especially under the present circumstances, but Solitaire had gotten as close as possible to keep an eye on Andrews. With carry-on bag in the overhead compartment, she was in an aisle seat behind the end of First Class with a diagonal view of the duo.

As the Flight Attendants made their before takeoff presentation, Solitaire went over her own checklist.

Once air born, flight time is roughly under three hours, depending upon the weather. The Consular agent doesn't look worried about anyone onboard while I only had time to run background checks on the crew scheduled for this trip.

The pilots were already secured in the cockpit, but it was a guess at best as to who among the passengers might be the incognito security agent on this flight since such information was never listed in any airline's computer system even if the flight provider knew in advance. The restroom attempt proved modern day safety logistics worked against whoever was behind this because weapons and potential suspects were more thoroughly screened by many countries since September 11, 2001.

The most likely scenario for another attempt was back in Miami, especially if anyone on the awaiting team was actually working for the other side.

As the plane started to taxi onto the runway, Andrews' guard turned to take a quick glance around.

The disguised Solitaire was looking out the window to her far left at the time but caught a glimpse of being stared at before the man turned to address Fredrick.

Wish I could hear what they're talking about, but I only have one listening device left and no opportunity to plant it without looking more suspicious than I might already be to him. But I wonder which one he is? All three went into the restroom yet I only know two by voice.

Oh well. Nothing to do but stay alert and be ready for whatever happens in Florida, Solitaire realized, settling in her seat as the craft picked up speed for takeoff.

+++

"I hate to think it might be an inside job, but I've ruled out every other possibility, including human error and mechanical malfunction," announced Ariel Andrews.

"They say two heads are better than one. I wish you would have let me help you," complained her assistant Carol Evans.

They had been back at Andrews Aviation since before four that afternoon but, other than a company security guard escort to the restrooms, none of the personnel from the drone demonstration had been allowed to leave their respective desks.

"Couldn't. This was something I had to do on my own."

Evans just sat in the guest chair and nodded as the head of Andrews Aviation continued recounting her investigation results, conducted at the air base and after their private jet's return flight to Miami.

"I verified the telemetry data. There is no indication that the technicians operating the prototype were involved or somehow managed to change the records to protect any accomplices before I could examine them. We were hacked. Someone simply flew the XDS-1 away."

"To where?"

"A nearby park off base where it could be retrieved quickly by someone waiting for it before a recovery team reached the scene," revealed the executive. "Security and I canvased the scene, but of course no one saw anything. Although local authorities have very few cameras in that area, I'm still waiting in hopes that the city honors my request for their Close Circuit Television footage. Yet even with the right equipment, what happened isn't possible without knowing the correct operating frequency, let alone the passwords to gain system access."

"So, you're suspecting industrial sabotage?" Carol cautiously asked, knowing who the guilty party was.

"Yes, but it certainly wasn't me or you," said Ariel.

It was all Evans could do to keep from breathing a sigh of relief. "Even if you've ruled out everyone onsite for the test today, that still leaves a lot of people involved in its development," she pointed out.

"I know, but we've got to get that drone back! The XDS-1 was meant for only civil and military law enforcement. In the wrong hands..."

The traitorous assistant's concentration on the executive's remarks was broken when she felt her muted cellphone vibrate within her jacket pocket. Yet there was no way Evans could check it now, let alone respond.

"So other than the food delivery I'm expecting any minute now, I'm having security lock down the complex for the night and giving everyone tomorrow off with pay while I personally continue looking into the situation."

"What?" Carol said, finally focusing again.

"I said 'Good Night Carol.'"

"Are you sure you don't need any help Ariel? I could—"

"Good Night, Ms. Evans," the executive repeated, a bit more coldly this time.

With that Carol reluctantly rose from her chair and left Andrews' office. She preferred to 'help' with the investigation in person but was confident Ariel would eventually discover the false trail of clues planted to accuse the patsy Evans set up to take the fall for the theft of both the prototype and its plans.

After Security confirmed Evans and everyone else had left Andrews Aviation and the food delivery was relayed to her office, the executive locked both the outer and inner doors. At her desk while chewing on a celery stick, Ariel took out a thick folder of documents from a drawer and started going through them again. *I know it had to be you, Carol. You're the only one, besides myself, with enough clearance to pull off everything that's been happening around here even before today. What I don't have is concrete confirmation of my suspicions and the reason why you'd betray me.*

Carol Evans drove away from the Andrews Aviation employee parking lot toward her home but stopped at a local shopping center first. There she let her convertible idle in a space while checking her cell and saw the familiar trio of question marks in a text from an unidentified sender. She deleted the message then made a call.

"It's me honey," Carol began once her boyfriend answered.

"I'm at your place," was all he said before hanging up.

A smile crossed her face as Evans rushed home to find César Fernandez lying naked in bed with a chilled bottle of champagne and two glasses nearby. *I know why you picked me to help with you schemes, but it does have some fringe benefits*, she thought with a smile while hastily getting undressed.

Their celebration was long and quite enjoyable for both.

Later, as they were cuddling, Carol told him, "I'm glad everything went well on your end, but we might have to deal with Ariel sooner than expected."

"No problem," he replied when she finished explaining. "The extra day together was unexpected but a nice bonus. Yet the time is drawing near for Reginald Andrews to face justice."

She agreed. "He promised to promote me before retiring, but his daughter hasn't." *I'm ten years older than her and should be more than just a personal assistant.*

"We both have our—" but that sentence remained unfinished as César's cellphone rang.

Carol didn't understand every Spanish word he spoke but saw Fernandez's mood change rapidly.

When César finished the call, she cautiously asked "Is something wrong?"

"Cancun went ca ca," he replied, before repeating what his employee reported.

"And your men?"

"Except for the one who called, they've all been arrested."

Fernandez saw the concerned look on Carol's face and added, "Don't worry. They're all loyal and know how to deal with the Policía down there. At least he managed to intercept the courier and brought the papers to Miami. But they're no good to me without—"

"Fredrick Andrews has to come home sometime, if he isn't already on his way," Carol reminded him.

"Si," César agreed with a smile. "I can arrange a special greeting for him," he added, before using his phone again.

First there was a text. Then he actually called someone. When that conversation was over, Fernandez turned and kissed her. "If not for you..." he began as they laid back down together.

"Don't worry mi querido. It may take time but in the end all our dreams will come true." *Especially mine,* she silently added.

+++

"From what I've heard that little thing sure beats the toy one my niño plays around with," Juan Juarez said, stretched out on a couch in the Anbessas' den to watch television.

"It sure does," agreed Alberto Aguilar from his chair at a nearby table. The brown-haired man was examining the XDS-1, satisfying his own curiosity about its design while following his leader's orders to make sure there was no way anyone could trace the stolen drone. "Its olfactory sensors alone..."

"¿Qué?"

"Its mechanical nose," Alberto said in simpler terms, forgetting that, unlike most of his amigos, he had graduated college before César Fernandez recruited him to be the Lions resident technical expert and oversee their weapons making enterprise. "What our Jefe has planned for this thing will soon make the Anbessas the top gang of all Miami." *What one man could do with this..*

+++

Anyone on the aircraft's right side could see the moon had fully risen above the horizon line. The Captain announced passengers needed to fasten their seat belts and secure all tray tables in preparation for the plane's impending landing.

During their journey the Consulate agent had turned his head a couple of more times Solitaire's way, as if bored and was just innocently taking in his surroundings. Each time he only saw Alistair Burke sitting in his seat listening to whatever was on his cellphone. The man never knew that the device was off, and she had been secretly keeping an eye on Fredrick Andrews and his escort, just in case.

Once the plane touched down and taxied to its designated terminal, the passengers disembarked in the order they boarded. Solitaire grabbed her carry-on bag from the overhead compartment, mentally prepared to face airport security with several possible contingency plans.

The line to Customs was single file and went straight from the plane, with the only deviation being upon reaching the secured screening area. Passengers went to either Clerk A and his assistant on the left or Clerk B and her partner on the right, depending upon who was the next available agent when your turn came.

Fredrick was several people ahead of her with the Consulate representative directly behind him. Solitaire took notice when the man from Cancun pulled out his cellphone. *Must have gotten a text now that all devices are out of airplane mode,* she realized, for he paused to type a reply before putting his phone away.

Solitaire caught a glimpse of Andrews' escort presenting identification, which allowed them the opportunity to be screened by Clerk A together. It didn't take long since neither had any luggage. That would have been examined before it was loaded onboard the plane and sent directly to the Baggage Claim area.

Both passed and left while the line moved tediously forward.

When her turn came, Solitaire presented Alistair Burke's credentials to Clerk B. The Clerk looked them over and asked a couple of routine questions while the assistant examined the carry on.

Then the new arrival was told he was free to go.

Solitaire was surprised to hear this but thanked the lady while grabbing her things and departed into the airport proper.

After all the fuss Hal made in Cancun over wanting to identify me and confirm if Juliet's team were officially sanctioned, something isn't adding up here. It could be that there isn't enough to detain me under any name for questioning, but I never take any chances.

With that thought Solitaire walked over to a time display and took out her cellphone. Various clocks showed the correct time in several major cities with all the individual time zones also indicated on the world map.

To the casual observer, Solitaire appeared like any other traveler checking their clock settings since, unlike most of the United States, Cancun didn't observe Daylight Savings Time.

Yet she was actually using the phone's camera to take a quick look at her surroundings.

Scanning the crowd revealed *There are a couple of possible suspects if someone plans to follow Alistair Burke in hopes I'll lead them to the rest of the 'team', but I can lose them easily enough once I'm out of the airport. Now what about this other group that is supposed to be meeting Andrews...*

Solitaire had almost finished casually sweeping the area via phone camera without being obvious about her actions, but stopped upon spotting a familiar face.

CHAPTER 16

*I*t's one of my playmates from Cancun! Solitaire realized, watching the man covertly keep an eye on Andrews and his companion from a distance. *Being a civilian with no government red tape to deal with, he easily could have taken an earlier flight and arrived before us. Yet unless he managed to get out of the janitor's closet and off the eighth floor before hotel security reached it, something's fishy.*

Solitaire was already moving to follow him while mentally taking stock of what she had available to work with because *even though this is a totally different disguise, it's at least partially compromised. Besides, he won't fall for the same trick again.*

The man was cautious, trailing his targets discretely from a distance. Never once losing sight of his quarry or letting them see him.

Still no sign of whoever was supposed to collect Andrews at the airport, Solitaire observed. *Could something have happened to them? Even if I had the frequency scanner app on this phone, there would be too many transmitted conversations going on at once to find the right one.*

Oblivious to the potential danger, Fredrick and his escort stopped in front of a men's room entrance. The duo looked like they were debating something.

Cancun paused and obscured his face by bending down as if to tie his shoe while Solitaire stopped to read the Flight Schedule board as the discussion continued.

Whatever the subject at hand, in the end Andrews entered the men's room alone while the agent stayed outside.

Cancun made a hasty approach toward the self-appointed sentry as Solitaire complained *Don't tell me he's going to attempt another restroom snatch.*

Instead, the two men stood in front of the entrance and started talking as if they were old friends unexpectedly bumping into each other.

Solitaire watched as they conversed. Both men were about the same height, although Cancun's more laid back, casual leisure suit allowed him to blend into a crowd better. He seemed anxious, even angrily pointing a finger at the facility during the conversation.

Consulate seemed hesitant about something. In the end they must have reached an agreement, for both now appeared calm. Then Cancun turned and left seconds before Andrews came back out.

With Fredrick blissfully unaware of his previous conversation, Consulate started talking to him again. Andrews simply nodded in agreement a couple of times before both turned and headed toward the closest exit.

The fact that Cancun now walked toward the same destination the moment the two were out of sight made Solitaire quicken her pace as well.

Still technically within the building, she stopped some steps behind the known enemy as he stood at the entrance and observed Consulate and Andrews traverse the crosswalk over to a nearby parking garage within the central confines of the main terminals.

Once they were inside, Cancun continued after them.

Contingency plans and other possibilities were running through her mind as the Covert Crusader crossed the final stretch of the encircling service road and entered the garage moments behind Cancun who, from a distance, saw the others get into an elevator before taking the stairs.

Solitaire raced behind him and caught the stairwell door before it completely closed.

She stood in the doorway and watched Cancun round the first midpoint landing on his way up, as if he already knew exactly what floor they were headed to and blissfully of being followed. With no time to see where the elevator's exterior level indicator would stop, she gave chase.

Although well-lit to offset the dull gray walls the staircase was narrow, barely large enough for two people to traverse it side by side. Solitaire kept to the staircase's far side to prevent the possibility of Cancun catching a glimpse of anyone else using this path should he happen to glance down while climbing.

The carry-on bag was slung over the right shoulder to prevent it scraping against the outer wall. Between that and the casual soft sole shoes of the Alistair Burke disguise, the noise risk was kept to a minimum as she hurried after her quarry as fast but as silently as possible.

Past the second floor access, Solitaire heard a noise. Cautiously rounding the next turn, she saw the third floor door closing. Since there was no indication of anyone still ascending, it had to be Cancun.

Moving faster now that the door was fully shut, Solitaire stood to one side of it and carefully peered through the small rectangular window above the door handle.

Cancun was off to her right, intently watching something from beside the front end of a parked pickup truck.

Solitaire completely pushed the handle downward before pulling the door slowly back just enough to stick her head through the newly created opening for a better view.

In the distance she saw Fredrick Andrews getting into the rear of a parked car as his escort joined whoever the driver was up front.

Upon seeing this, Cancun turned and headed off to his right. But why was he smiling?

Trailing after him, Solitaire took a quick peek and saw the other car still sitting in its space. *Were they waiting for Cancun?*

Her suspect was parked a distance away from Andrews' transport. Despite the upper levels not having as much wide-open space as the ground floor and this unit of the airport's overall garage complex barely being half full on a week night, the sports car he stopped in front of would go unnoticed among the other performance cars present unless you were specifically looking for it.

Yet Cancun had a good line of sight on Fredrick. *Sheer dumb luck or something else?*

Cancun had picked a far corner to park in, with no visible Closed Circuit Security Cameras. After a quick look revealed there were no potential witnesses in the area, Solitaire ran as fast as she could to cover the last few feet between them before throwing herself against Cancun as if she was tackling a rival football player.

Having pulled a key ring from his pants pocket, Cancun was about to click the fob button to unlock the door when the man was suddenly slammed against the driver's side of the auto before two arms went around his neck.

The key ring fell to the concrete flooring as he tried to pry the offending limbs off, which caused his opponent to further tighten their grip. Unable to prevent his attacker from applying the choke hold, Cancun moved to dislodge his assailant by body slamming them against the car.

Solitaire relaxed everything but her arms to mimic a limp rag doll, but still felt the intense shock of hitting the car back first.

A bit dazed but still hanging on, Solitaire moved her legs in an attempt to trip her opponent as Cancun took a step forward to make another ramming attempt.

The man stumbled and tried to right himself even as the side of his head hit the car frame above the driver's window.

Solitaire managed to twist her body enough to put Cancun between her and the vehicle, making sure the choke hold remained tightly applied in the process.

Yet the man refused to yield as he switched tactics and suddenly started falling backwards, hoping to trap his attacker between himself and the parking garage floor.

Despite hating to let go, Solitaire released the choke hold and tumbled to her right. She moved quickly to assume a new position to continue the fight, but it was unnecessary.

Unable to stop himself, Cancun landed head first upon the concrete. Between that and the effects of the choke hold, the man had lost the fight.

After making sure he was still alive and breathing, Solitaire turned him onto one side and used the detachable shoulder strap from the carry-on bag to secure Cancun's arms tightly behind his back at the wrists.

She found the key ring lying on the ground slightly under and behind the left front tire. After opening the door, she briefly considered dragging the unconscious man into the back seat but there was no time to spare.

Solitaire had figured out what was going on and needed to rescue Fredrick Andrews again.

CHAPTER 17

The other car was beginning to back out of its space as Solitaire hastily tossed her bag inside and threw on the seat belt before starting Cancun's vehicle. *Were they just ready to go or had they seen any of the fight and are now attempting to escape?*

The answer came as she started pulling out; the sound of tires speeding up echoed in the confining space of the parking garage. *Damn! They did catch enough of the fight to realize something was wrong!*

Solitaire turned the corner and sped across the straight away that led to the access ramps which allowed vehicles to change floors.

Taking the down ramp faster than the posted speed limit, she managed to catch up to her quarry without another automobile coming between them. They were now practically bumper to bumper.

She could see the driver say something to the Consulate Agent while Andrews looked over his shoulder out the rear windshield. Although still disguised as Alistair Burke, Solitaire gave what she hoped was a reassuring wave. Whatever Fredrick's opinion might be, he turned around to face forward again.

Upon reaching the lowest level, both cars were in line to check out of the parking garage. There were others ahead of them, but Solitaire managed to stay right behind her target despite the driver switching lanes for an alternate booth at the last moment without signaling and an audible protest from the pickup that originally would have been behind them instead of her cutting it off.

She wanted to intercept once outside and keep them confined on airport property. This presented the best opportunity to rescue and escape with Andrews rather than making an attempt now and risk being trapped within the garage.

However, fate had other plans.

The last car before Andrews' had just paid their fee. The boom barrier was rising to allow that vehicle's departure when Fredrick rolled down his passenger side window and started yelling "HELP! They're trying to kidnap me!"

That brief statement got instant action as a couple of security guards, from positions around the collection booths and exit, came running toward the car.

Fredrick kept shouting even as the driver raised the window back up. Despite repeated attempts, Solitaire could see Andrews failing to get out of the car. *The auto maker's child proof locks are probably active to keep the doors secured, since the rear windows never go low enough to prevent anyone from trying to climb out.*

From behind, it looked to Solitaire like the Consulate Agent now had his credentials in hand and was about to attempt smooth talking his way out of the mess he found himself in.

Instead, the driver hit the gas and sped through the opening. The bottom of the lowering barrier scraped across the top of their roof as the vehicle fled the parking garage.

Although on foot, the guards attempted to give chase. While they would lose the car in a matter of seconds, at least they could get the license plate and a partial description of the occupants.

Solitaire's response was to stomp on the gas pedal of her borrowed vehicle.

The gate arm was back in place, but now slightly bent.

Yet that didn't matter as she crashed through with horn blaring to warn anyone in her path to get out of the way.

Not slowing down, Solitaire turned into outbound traffic leaving the airport terminals, almost side swiping a taxi in the process.

Well into the late hours of the evening, individual vehicle headlights joined all the street lights and other illumination sources along the way.

The airport exit road ran parallel with and provided access to the divided street from which Miami International derived its formal address. There was also a service road ahead that led to some smaller side roads for supporting businesses as well as traditional commercial enterprises the farther one got away from the airport proper.

Plenty of opportunities for escape before reaching the highway bordering the airport and its variables entered the picture.

Without trying to draw attention to herself, Solitaire continued following the other car while looking for a chance to overtake them safely.

She observed whoever drove that vehicle frantically dodging and weaving through the three lanes of outbound traffic. Several horn blares and a few hand gestures indicated her fellow motorists weren't happy with the idiot among them, but so far there were no mishaps. While she followed a similar course, Solitaire kept signaling when appropriate and time permitted.

There currently were no flashing lights in her rear view and side mirrors heralding additional pursuit, but she figured it was just a matter of time unless airport security and local authorities had established a roadblock somewhere ahead. *At least whoever is interested in Fredrick still wants him alive. Maybe the police will be able to handle this themselves without my involvement.*

What glimpses Solitaire had of him showed Fredrick Andrews still trying to escape. After failing to open either passenger door or break its window with his bare hands, a desperate but futile effort to begin with, she was shocked to see him reach out from the back seat and attack the driver!

The car started swaying in and out of lanes uncontrollably. Other drivers tried their best, but not all managed to prevent having some kind of accident. Most were either colliding with guard rails or jumping the curb into the bordering landscaped medians, but some wound up crashing into another traveler and damaging both vehicles.

So far, she had managed to avoid every obstacle unscathed while not losing sight of the target, but still had no chance for a totally clean intercept. From her position behind them, Solitaire saw the Consulate Agent try to steer from the passenger side as the driver and Andrews continued fighting.

Fredrick had the driver in a choke hold that his opponent attempted to escape, but the battle was brief as they crashed into the rear of a delivery van!

Solitaire parked as close as safety allowed behind the scene while throwing on her car's hazard flashers.

With only the far left one still open, traffic was seriously slowing down from being forced into a single lane. Leaving all the doors unlocked and the key in the ignition with the engine idling, Solitaire got out with her bag and rushed over to the wreck.

The delivery van was in the slow lane, within viewing distance of the next overpass. The car with Andrews had crashed into it at an angle from the middle lane. Their right front was seriously damaged at least to the tire well. The wheel itself was bent at an odd angle toward the nearby curb.

Through the steam rising from under the dented hood and broken grill work, Solitaire could see a hint of police vehicle light bars shining brightly against the night sky from either shoulder, indicating that the roadblock she predicted began at the top of the overpass, well pass the service road exit. She surmised traffic would have been funneled toward the middle lane as it went down the other side, surrounded by officers. Yet now everyone was either on their radios or moving their transports out of the way to respond to the accident, which didn't give her much time.

Of more importance were the car's occupants.

The driver and the Consulate Agent were both unconscious. The front seat airbags had deployed, so Solitaire couldn't see much of either man below the shoulders, but both looked like they were still breathing.

She then took a few steps to her left and looked for Andrews. Fredrick was lying across the back seat. His head laid against the door behind the driver but faced the passenger side as he moaned.

"Are you all right?" she called out in a male voice.

"I—" he began, trying to focus on the man at the car window.

I don't see any blood, but he might have a concussion or internal injuries, realized Solitaire.

"Don't move. Help is on the way," the stranger told Andrews. "Can you tell me what happened?"

He looked at the man through the right passenger window and tried to focus.

"T-thought it odd when no one rode with me in back, but Barry said they were short-handed," Fredrick began, putting a name to the Consulate Agent. "I knew something was wrong when they got spooked about... you!" he shouted, his vision finally clearing. "Who?"

"Juliet says hello."

While still stationary, that statement made Fredrick more alert than anything else Solitaire could have said. "How do I know you're truly with her?" Andrews asked, not bothering to first say anything along the lines of "Juliet who?"

"Perdóneme. ¿Conoces el camino a San José?" Solitaire answered in perfect Spanish, but using Alistair Burke's male voice instead of the feminine one from that alias.

Andrews eyes grew wide in both comprehension and understanding as Solitaire said, "One of your Cancun playmates is tied up on the third floor of the parking garage, but the next time someone asks you to remain silent about the agency, please do so!"

With a quick glance to her right, Solitaire added, "Now I've got to go," running away from the scene before the closest of the first responders arrived.

CHAPTER 18

With neither time to retrieve the car she was using nor a viable route to drive, Solitaire fled on foot because the authorities would have a lot of questions that had to remain unanswered.

Police cars with officers running alongside them were traveling the wrong way down either shoulder to reach the accident scene.

Andrews called out. Whether for help in general or the stranger who knew Juliet specifically didn't matter. Solitaire paid him no heed and jumped the concrete barrier. Thankfully from that point it was a short fall to the landscaped area left open by the airport planners.

Scrambling back to her feet, she ran for there was no time to collect the hair dye remover and at least a fresh shirt to attempt altering her appearance.

Other voices shouting from her departure point demanded whoever the stranger was to stop and return, but the unidentified Person of Interest now wanted for questioning kept moving away from the scene.

The surrounding street lights and distant buildings provided enough illumination to see by as she ran a course parallel to the nearby road through what reminded Solitaire of the rough or bunker from some country club's golf course.

She never looked back to confirm possible pursuit, for that would waste precious seconds. With a good head start, her destination was in sight.

Solitaire risked jaywalking across the street, dodging what cars were on the road this late in the evening to reach the other side. Even with the road signs indicating location, it still surprised her for there to be a bus station so relatively close to a major airport, but she wasn't going to look a proverbial gift horse in the mouth.

The bus company shared the property with another business, so it took Solitaire a moment to spot an entrance for the station. The plan had been to dash inside, find a convenient restroom and do a quick change, but—

Damn! Someone radioed ahead, she cursed, for three uniformed security guards came out of the depot as she approached. The trio looked around to get their bearings then, spotting the suspect, gave chase.

Going to the right was not feasible. Besides it not making much sense to head back toward the airport and risk increased security, the airplanes parked on the adjoining property behind a high fence proved there would be no opportunities for hiding, let alone escape.

Solitaire turned left and kept running.

Although there was no sign of any patrol cars in pursuit, that could soon change. The only thing working in her favor were the long stretches of road bordering the large areas of land required for airport functions and services.

There was an aviation fuel storage facility on Solitaire's right past the bus station. On the left was something that might be its employee parking area. However, there was no chance to duck in there unseen, leaving the only option to continue running down the road toward the hint of a freeway overpass in the distance.

There had not been any sign of motorists in the last few moments, but the sound of pursuing footsteps was growing louder. Keeping pace with her rapid breathing and the increased beating of her heart.

Did that mean more police had joined the chase or were they getting closer?

Solitaire had been running at her full potential from the start. It had only been a couple of minutes and just over a mile so far by her estimate yet, while an avid jogger in good health, even she would need a rest break soon.

The tall security fence surrounding the fuel reserves seemed endless.

Up ahead lay another intersection but, from what she could see, vehicles could only go left or right with no direct connection to her goal. The freeway was still visible, yet well behind an electrical substation and a lot more open ground.

Then Solitaire heard a noise.

With no actual sidewalk to use, she had been running alongside the road's rough concrete gutter and hoped not to be hit by a passing car while trying to avoid apprehension.

Solitaire risked looking back and saw someone driving an open bed pickup truck slowing down to turn left at the intersection, totally ignoring the scene they were now passing.

There was also at least one police officer only a few feet away, keeping pace with their as yet unidentified suspect. He wasn't alone, but the others were noticeably behind him.

With an adrenaline fueled burst of speed, she changed course. Another car had to slam on its brakes to avoid hitting the madman running out into the street.

Solitaire managed to hop onto its rear bumper just as the truck turned. Both hands grasped the rusty top of the tailgate, the carry-on bag the only buffer between it and her left.

Looking over her shoulder, Solitaire saw the other car turn right and the officers who had been chasing her gather on the side of the road to regroup. Yet while they had given up the race, at least one was on their radio to update the rest of the police in the area.

Although now headed back toward where law enforcement was staging the start of their roadblock, at least this direction presented new chances to leave the area without anyone discovering the secrets of the Solitaire program.

The pickup driver seemed oblivious to having a passenger, let alone the other vehicle's horn of protest from when Solitaire made her desperate dash. His head was bobbing up and down to something on the truck's radio. Despite the fact she saw him crank up the volume to enjoy the broadcast, Solitaire still couldn't make out what was playing with the cab windows rolled up. Between that and the background noises from her current method of travel, it was a small wonder she heard anything from his speakers at all with the truck's air conditioner on.

As they approached the first of two consecutive overpasses, Solitaire stood while still holding onto the tail gate. A few police cars remained parked on its outbound shoulder as their officers dealt with the accident. She jumped from her unsuspecting ride as the truck entered the open space before the second overpass.

Her right foot landed on top of one of the waist high concrete traffic barriers aligned to denote the route's outer edge. Then she instantly used it as a spring board to clear that hurdle, with the left foot landing first upon solid ground again.

Solitaire went limp and rolled right. Momentum added from the moving vehicle carried her to the base of a railroad track that ran parallel to the road.

She stopped on her back at the edge of the rail's raised gravel ballast bed.

Not wasting a second Solitaire rose and, staying crouched low to avoid being spotted, crossed the tracks then raced up the embankment on the other side.

Using a large grouping of tall shrubs for cover, Solitaire briefly stopped to peer through the foliage and saw the flashing lights of a roadblock on the road beyond the second overpass, stopping the pickup before it reached the next intersection.

It won't take the police long to figure out what happened and resume searching for me.

With time of paramount importance, she crossed the scenic landscaping to a circular off ramp from the freeway, then went beyond it into another open but well-maintained area. This section appeared to be patterned on a golf course motif too, but with a couple of pseudo sand traps bordered by woods.

When necessary, Solitaire had her cellphone to navigate the terrain but only used its touch screen's glow to see by instead of the brighter flashlight app to avoid drawing unwanted attention.

As she crossed a large patch of wood mulch to cautiously draw closer to the freeway's feeder road, Solitaire stayed low and observed the scene before her.

To the left was nothing but a gigantic concrete cloverleaf of highway, bordered by lots of additional scenic landscaping to appease the tourists.

To her right was an open business.

Some kind of restaurant or night club, she realized. The echo of a quick music beat could be heard while the breeze carried the faint whiff of a delicious smell, which reminded Solitaire how long it had been since her last meal.

A quick glance at Alistair Burke's wristwatch revealed it was close to eleven.

....then raced up the embankment...

The disguised Discrete Defender stood and started walking toward the establishment.

Approaching from the rear, Solitaire saw that the building sat at an angle in relation to its surroundings. The front facade fully faced the feeder road and its far-left outer wall the highway. That major artery diagonally passed the Fiesta Cantina, for a large and well-lit mural bragging about the business covered the whole wall, visible to any who drove by. Other than a few strategically placed plants growing out of a small bed of gravel along the foundation, the rest of that side was open land.

Exterior lights that indicated the kitchen and delivery entrances along the back wall were dim compared to those illuminating the parking lot on the right-hand side of the property.

Transportation was key to escaping the authorities, let alone getting to where she needed to be next. Solitaire had no problem reusing the vehicle of someone against her, but if it became necessary to commandeer a civilian's transportation, full yet clandestine restitution would somehow eventually be made to the owner.

There were no noticeable surveillance cameras, but that didn't mean the place was unprotected. A guard could be keeping an eye on a monitor somewhere inside or some employee might come out on an errand or break, so Solitaire walked around the mural side to the front and hoped no one saw her before entering the public area.

Prepared to say she just wanted a good look at the mural if anyone spotted her, Solitaire turned the corner and saw a possible solution to her dilemma.

CHAPTER 19

The entry lane from the service road took vehicles along a curve that ran parallel with the front of the building until it reached an oversized portico on the far side, for those who wanted to use the cantina's valet service, before leading to the parking area.

As Solitaire came around the corner, she spotted a taxi signaling its intention to turn onto the property and ran to intercept before the cab could reach the front door and whoever actually summoned it.

Uncertain where he came from, the driver stopped upon seeing a man flag him down as he pulled in. Despite appearing a little disheveled, the stranger was dressed well enough, but why was one hand holding a small yellow bag? Concerned, the driver reached back for the handgun hidden in its rear holster attached to his belt between body and seat cushion as the stranger approached the front passenger side window.

"Thank heavens you're here," Solitaire began in a male voice with a Southern accent as the driver used his left hand to electronically lower the window just enough for conversation. "The ambulance took my brother away a little while ago. They think his appendix is about to burst. Joe's wife went with him, and I was supposed to follow in their car, but it wasn't until I got to the parking lot that I remembered he drove here and still has his keys on him."

Well, that explains his anxiousness and meeting me so soon, thought the driver, but still...

"Name?" the cab operator asked.

"I'm not sure who made the call on my behalf. I just came back from Georgia, and we stopped here to eat after they picked me up from the airport," lied Solitaire, while pulling out a wallet. "I'm Alistair Burke," she said, showing the cab driver her false Florida identification, "and this will be on top of whatever the fare comes to if you take me to the hospital," briefly displaying a fifty-dollar bill before sticking it back in the wallet.

Like any hard-working stiff, the driver would have preferred a higher denomination, but wasn't going to turn down a tip. "Hop in back," he said, unlocking the rear passenger door remotely while using his right to activate the ride meter. At least for now, the handgun wouldn't be needed.

Solitaire hurried inside and the cab circled around to get back on the feeder road, never going to the cantina's front entrance. She took one brief look out the window as they drove way but didn't see anyone searching for their missing ride.

The cab driver stayed on the feeder road and radioed his dispatcher that the fare was picked up and their destination.

The taxi turned at the next intersection to head back toward Miami and the closest hospital to their location.

Able to relax for a moment, Solitaire started going through the carry-on bag. There were still a couple of polo style shirts and another pair of pants inside to help alter her appearance. Of more importance was the hair dye remover, disguised as an unopened bottle of mouthwash.

Yet there was something else within the toiletries case as well. It was a flat disc, smaller and thinner than a dime. Solid black, totally smooth to the touch and perfectly round. If not for the fact that Solitaire knew all of her possessions by both sight and touch, she may not have discovered it in the dim light of the cab's interior.

Doesn't look audio capable. A tracking device? Solitaire recalled the only time the bag was briefly out of her control and realized, *So that's why I got through Customs easier than I thought I might. Whatever Federal Agency this belongs to had it hidden in my bag, hoping I'd lead them to the rest of the 'Cancun team'. If it belonged to the local police, I'd already be in custody.*

With that she lowered the passenger window just long enough to toss the device out of the car onto the highway. The fact they were passing the Fiesta Cantina on the opposite side made her smile. *Even when they realize I ditched their tracker, they'll think I managed to cross the freeway and keep looking for me out here.*

"Everything all right back there?" the driver wondered.

"Yeah. Just had to get rid of a bug that was bothering me," his passenger answered.

"Good. I try to run a clean cab," the driver said. Then his right hand drifted back near the hidden handgun before he spoke again. "If you don't mind me asking, what's with the bag?"

"The food's great, but unfortunately the shorts and T-shirt I flew home in weren't up to the cantina's dress code. Joe got my bag out of his trunk so I could change clothes in their restroom, but none of us saw the point of taking the time to put it back in the car."

"Bummer," replied the driver, thinking of the comfortable summer attire he currently had on as his hand drifted away from the gun again.

Would have been surprised if you didn't ask about it, since I realized the discrepancy in my hastily made story, observed Solitaire. *I certainly don't want you using that weapon you're hiding behind your back.*

+++

Although Solitaire discretely checked every once in a while to make sure she wasn't being followed, the rest of the journey was uneventful.

The cab pulled into the hospital property and parked near the Visitors Entrance to the Emergency area.

The passenger got out and paid the driver, including the promised fifty.

Yet as the cab started to pull away, Solitaire acted like she had just received a call on her cellphone and stopped to answer it. This kept the driver from seeing that his customer didn't go directly inside.

With no one else nearby, Solitaire pantomimed having a conversation while taking in her surroundings.

Across the street from the hospital was a line of businesses. Most were closed for the night, except for a 24-hour diner and a gasoline vending convenience store with the same operating schedule.

Despite being so good at it, I'm getting tired of the restroom quick change, silently complained Solitaire as she walked away from the hospital after confirming the cab had left.

Can't take the risk of anyone inside seeing me like this in case security or whatever cops are guarding Andrews are still on the lookout for me, she realized, while waiting for the crosswalk light to turn in her favor. *Still using the Burke identity is a risk I'll have to take a little longer, but not having another ID physically with me is an oversight I'll have to correct in the future, once I figure out how to get extra credentials through airport security.*

With that a lone pedestrian crossed the street. *Better use the convenience store if I can because I might need the diner later.*

The gas station was in a prime location, so another customer entering the busy store went virtually unnoticed.

Solitaire walked straight to the back and locked herself in the men's room. A few minutes later a totally different gentleman came out. If anyone was actually paying attention, the same yellow carry-on bag was the only clue as to what occurred.

Gone was the dark hair in favor of her own natural color. Not wanting to tie up the restroom for too long in case someone else needed it, she kept everything from the waist down. The eye color changing contact lenses were back within their protective case, but now inside a pants pocket. The false finger print applications stayed in place as a necessity because Solitaire didn't want her own on file anywhere. She donned a fresh men's shirt, complete with a new compliment of sleeping gas filled buttons.

Stopping only long enough to pay cash for a bottle of water and a couple of granola bars, Solitaire quickly left the convenience store and walked back to the street. There she paused at a bus stop a half block down to check the posted schedule while eating the food. The fact that the next bus wouldn't be there until after sunrise was no surprise.

Before leaving, the Secret Samaritan put the empty wrappers in an overfilled trash can, then dropped the carry-on bag and kicked it under the bench provided for waiting bus riders. *Hopefully someone in need will find it, but there's nothing in there that can be traced back to me that I still need nor can't replace, considering I removed all the gas buttons from the other shirts and have them in the pocket of the one I'm wearing.* With only three at most on any polo shirt, the clothing would still be wearable despite not being able to button the placket.

With unfinished water bottle still in hand, Solitaire went back to the crosswalk and waited for the light to return to the hospital and check on Fredrick Andrews.

CHAPTER 20

After dumping the now empty bottle in a recycling bin outside, Solitaire discretely eyed everything and everyone as she entered the Emergency section of the hospital.

The nurses all wore the same style of teal scrubs. Doctors only had white lab coats with the hospital logo over the left pocket, worn over regular clothing. The place was ordered chaos. All were busy trying to treat everyone, based upon priority of need.

Solitaire observed the waiting area was overflowing with people as she stood in line before the front desk. Every chair held someone while others either slumped on the floor or leaned against any available wall space. She was uncertain how many were actually seeking help versus just accompanying a potential patient.

There were a couple of security guards in gray uniforms stationed at strategic positions, watching everything. Yet none seemed to be interested in or assigned to a specific person at the moment.

An ambulance would have come directly from the accident. Considering my delay getting here, they might have already moved Fredrick to a hopefully private room after treatment, she surmised. *Yet if I ask for him directly, that would raise too many red flags, so—*

"Can I help you?" the lady at the Emergency Room's Check-In Station asked the next person standing before her counter. While not a nurse herself, she was wearing a vest and name tag that indicated hospital employment.

"My baby's having a sister. I mean, my sister is having a baby. I'm going to be an uncle!" Solitaire happily exclaimed, using a previous male voice, but one different than what the cab driver heard.

"Well, congratulations," the clerical aide behind the counter said. "Your first time?"

"Is it that obvious?" Solitaire asked with a grin.

"Kind of," the aide replied with a smile, thankful this one was easy to handle before giving directions to the Maternity Ward.

Solitaire walked past all the people waiting for assistance toward a connecting corridor, but was stopped by a security guard before she could leave the Emergency area.

"I need you to stand within that blue taped square on the floor so I can take your temperature. Then you need to show me some identification before I can let you pass," the woman at the checkpoint informed the visitor.

"Certainly," the disguised Solitaire replied as she entered the square.

After a mechanical voice announced, "Temperature normal," the Clandestine Crusader pulled out a wallet and displayed Alistair Burke's ID, but kept her finger over the top of the photo to prevent showing that the hair color now didn't match.

"Just a moment," the guard said, while she pushed a button on her computer.

Solitaire briefly considered possible escape scenarios before hearing the telltale sound of a thermal printer behind the guard's desk.

"Here you are," the woman said, handing Solitaire a temporary Visitors' Pass with a grainy black and white photo of her disguise on it. "Go right on ahead and sir?"

"Yes?" Solitaire wondered.

"Congratulations."

+++

The hallway was short and presented no opportunities for Solitaire to carry out her current mission.

At the end was another security station. Despite the late hour, the guard there didn't seem that concerned about the new arrival since they had already been cleared.

As she continued on her way towards Maternity, Solitaire paused to look at a copy of the building directory attached to one wall, more to see what might be available than to pretend the hospital's latest visitor needed to verify still being on course. *All I need is a few minutes at most alone with a computer to check on Andrews' status. Unfortunately Administration is on another floor and Emergency was too well manned, hence picking a hopefully more vulnerable target.*

Past the double doors that separated her destination from the rest of the hospital, Solitaire saw nothing but a solid wall on the left and one lone door in the middle of the right-hand wall before some interior windows. A few steps forward confirmed that area being Maternity's Waiting Room. A quick peek through the glass revealed two anxious fathers sitting impatiently inside.

Ahead was the Nurses' Station. Behind the off-white counter was an office door, partially open but its interior lights off.

Traffic could only turn left here, for to the right was another solid wall. The station was placed in such a way that no one could pass without notice, although there was a small gap between it and the wall for egress. The main staff access point was on the opposite end.

The nurses' area behind the counter was covered with charts. The public side had instructional posters concerning how to properly care for your newborn in both English and Spanish.

Of more importance were the security cameras. One was mounted in each upper corner, but both aimed toward the left and angled to not take in much of the station itself. *Must be where the nursery is, with the new mothers recovering somewhere beyond it,* surmised Solitaire.

She had walked quietly since entering. The rapid use of a keyboard could be heard the closer Solitaire drew near, so it took a moment for the lady behind the counter to look up from her computer and realize anyone was there.

"Oh. Sorry. Busy night," the nurse said by way of apology. "Can I help you?"

"Yes, I–" Solitaire began but was interrupted by another nurse appearing in the hall further away from the station.

"Sandy, can you give me a hand?" requested the new arrival. "Debra is still in Delivery. I'm busy with one and another just started crying."

"I'll be right back," promised the nurse, before rising from the chair to help her partner.

"Take your time. They're more important," Solitaire replied, jumping at the opportunity. *This is far better than any plan I had come up with so far.*

The moment the uniformed women were out of sight, Solitaire went behind the counter through the opening on the right. While one hand removed her cellphone from the pants pocket it currently occupied, the other used the keyboard to switch work screens and look for Fredrick Andrews.

Not knowing how much time she might have, Solitaire took phone photos the instant the requested information appeared onscreen.

Once the computer was reset to where the nurse had it, Solitaire went back to the public side of the counter and looked over the information.

Some contusions and bruising. No internal injuries. Dazed at admittance. Somewhat alert and aware as time went on but they're holding Fredrick at least overnight for observation under standard concussion protocols. Private room on the fifth floor, with an armed guard and instructions to notify both the local police and FBI before he's discharged. Whatever is going on, they want to give him a proper and safe escort home this time, with hopefully no traitors in that detail.

With research done the incriminating evidence was deleted. Then Solitaire held the phone like she was in the middle of a conversation yet never spoke until Sandy reappeared.

"What do you mean I'm at the wrong hospital?" Solitaire paused before saying "Oh. Well, I'll be there as soon as possible. Give Sis my love," and pretended to end the call.

"Sorry about that," the visitor said to the returning employee. "I came here when Joe called me and said my sister went into labor because this is the closest hospital to their house, but he never told me they were out when it happened, so they went to the one closer to the movie theater. Otherwise, it's a niece and I'm an uncle."

"Congratulations," Sandy replied, unaware of the subterfuge.

As the visitor turned to walk away, Solitaire's last thought before leaving the Maternity Ward was *Someday.*

CHAPTER 21

S olitaire grabbed a couple of spare buttons out of her shirt pocket as she walked through the double doors and turned left instead of going right for the closest exit.

Under the belief of trust but verify, the plan was to make it upstairs and check on Andrews for herself before leaving the hospital.

Unfortunately, the security guard who just entered the otherwise deserted hallway from a door up ahead had other ideas. Seeing a stranger in an unauthorized area, he rapidly approached his target.

This man wasn't the sentry from the last check point. Solitaire observed a swagger in his walk, right hand resting on top of the security uniform's utility belt near his sidearm like an Old West cowboy prepared to draw. Of course, this also put his handcuffs and pepper spray within reach too.

Better make this quick. I have no idea where all the surveillance cameras are, and I certainly don't want a prolonged fight.

"Oh, thank God I finally found one of you guys," she said, using the same male voice everyone in the hospital had heard so far. "There's some idiot in the Maternity Ward accusing the nurses of switching babies!"

"What?" said the guard in disbelief, but before he could respond to the situation, a green gas erupted from the palm of the stranger's left hand.

Still holding her breath, Solitaire grabbed the now unconscious man before he could hit the ground and dragged him into the recently left room. While there was no exterior sign indicating what was within, the contents made her smile.

Supplies! The guard must have just been making his rounds because there's nothing important in here that needs to be seriously regulated, like pharmaceuticals. However there's more than enough for me to work with, happily thought Solitaire as she grabbed a brand-new doctor's jacket off a shelf, still pristine in its manufacturer's plastic wrapper.

A few moments later the being a few knew as an expecting uncle emerged from the supply room, but noticeably different in appearance. Solitaire had carefully removed the hospital visitor's pass and placed it within her wallet in case another need for it arose. The white lab coat didn't do much to cover the bit of extra body weight she now allegedly carried because of what was hidden underneath, secured by the polo shirt being tucked in. A bit of sterile cotton wadding within each cheek added to the illusion of being overweight.

Too bad I couldn't find any name tags, she mused. *The pens in the jacket pocket, metal storage clipboard filled with various blank forms and stethoscope draped around my neck ready for action do support the doctor image though.*

With the new disguise as complete as it could be for spur of the moment, the alleged hospital employee walked over to the closest elevator.

The ride to the fifth floor was brief and uneventful.

As the elevator doors opened Solitaire was already in character, looking intently at whatever important document was on top of the pile within the clipboard.

Still, no detail of her surroundings went unnoticed. A quick but discrete peek through the door glass of the waiting area across from the elevator revealed it to be currently empty. Rectangular shaped, the room was much smaller than Maternity's, with the short end's door side and its opposing wall.

Being at the far end of a long hallway since she didn't use the main elevator, the walk to the Nurses' Station proved every room was private. With most having their doors slightly ajar, the various views confirmed each was just large enough for a single patient in bed and whatever medical equipment they might need.

Yet only one had a guard posted outside.

The doctor casually assumed a position at the counter that would not to be in anyone's way, still lost in whatever paperwork had his attention. Yet the Secret Samaritan had a clear view of Fredrick Andrews' room and kept a discrete eye on it while maintaining her charade.

The uniformed police officer outside the closed door was alert, watching everyone present. Yet there was nothing visible that required his immediate attention.

The public elevator faced the Nurses' Station on its right. There were only a few more patient rooms to the sentry's left. This side of the fifth floor ended a few feet past Solitaire with a supply area and a break room, for she could see another doctor inside through the partially open door.

She knew better than to attempt gaining entry to see Andrews, so settled for waiting until someone authorized did. Not knowing his room's interior arrangement, she hoped that it would allow a quick peek of him through the open door.

For all I know, he could be sound asleep with the privacy curtain closed, or worse. This could all be a decoy and Fredrick is actually somewhere else, she realized. *Everyone has been letting the doctor work in peace so far, but I can't stay in this one spot for too long without somebody getting suspicious, so I better start scouting alternate locations.*

That was when the elevator behind her chimed that its car had arrived. As the doors opened, Solitaire noticed the man get off and turned right. He looked at Andrews room for a moment while the guard stared at him.

The new arrival had black hair, was a few inches taller than her and more muscular, judging by the arms appearing a bit tight in the sleeves of the jacket over his casual attire. He carried a bouquet of flowers and appeared lost in the corridor.

"Visiting hours are-" the guard began.

"I know, but my wife was brought here earlier tonight after a traffic accident and I just got off work a little while ago, so they let me come up," claimed the new arrival.

The guard simply nodded as the man took a look at the card within the bouquet and started to turn right, before changing directions to traverse the corridor Solitaire had already traveled. She couldn't make out the name on the visitor's pass and didn't recognize him but instinctively knew something wasn't quite right.

Especially when he slowed down a step while passing Andrews' door, as if contemplating his options with the guard outside.

He walked out of sight beyond the Nurses' Station, but Solitaire now followed quietly a few steps behind the flower carrier.

The visitor stopped in front of one door, as if contemplating going inside. Yet Solitaire knew that room was empty. Then the man went to the end of the hall and entered the waiting room.

As the door closed, Solitaire moved closer to the entrance. Her left hand was on the doorknob, the right held the clipboard. The man's back filled the open window space. She cocked her head to one side, bringing the left ear closer to the partition while keeping an eye on the guard. If he happened to look her way, it appeared as if the doctor was double checking his notes before entering the waiting room.

A moment later she heard the man talking to someone in Spanish.

"No es factible. Está demasiado bein protegido." a deep voice said. In English, "It's not doable. He's too well guarded."

Unfortunately, the other half of his phone conversation was inaudible.

Solitaire hoped to hear more, but there was only a brief pause before a "Si," followed by an "Adios."

With the guard not looking her way as he made another visual scan of his surroundings, Solitaire turned the knob and forced her way inside.

"¿Qué—" the man started to say as the door pressed against his back. Caught off guard, he found himself trapped between it and the wall with only his left arm and cellphone free.

Solitaire knew he wouldn't stay contained for long as she pressed against the door with all her might.

"Hablar," she said angrily in a different male voice, demanding the man talk.

With right hand palm flat against the wall as the flowers fell to the floor, his response was to push back against the door.

Solitaire was prepared for the escape attempt and had already moved to her left. The door's outer trim barely brushed the far edge of the lab coat as it swung shut.

"Loco medico," the man growled as his right fist moved to punch Solitaire in the face, but his bare knuckles hit the metal clipboard she held defensively with both hands as her right knee struck the tender spot between her opponent's legs.

He took a step back. Solitaire guessed why as she pressed on with her impromptu inquiry. "¿Quién está detrás de Andrews?" she asked, wanting to know who was after Andrews.

The man remained silent while trying to punch her in the stomach.

Solitaire moved back a step to avoid the blow and brought the metal clipboard down hard on top of his head.

He staggered but refused to fall as she extracted a couple of spare buttons from her shirt pocket.

Dazed, his blurry vision couldn't make out what the doctor might have grabbed but instinct made him swat at Solitaire's left hand, which sent the buttons flying across the waiting room.

"Okay. We do this the hard way," she replied in English, taking a defensive stance.

The man just smiled as if he understood and then charged at her.

Given the room's small size and shape, there were only a few feet to move around in.

Solitaire went toward her right instead of left this time and the man missed his target completely. He crashed into the wall headfirst, his body slumping into the cheap chair beneath him to reveal cracked sheet rock at the point of impact.

Her opponent stirred once in a feeble attempt to rise but failed.

She approached him cautiously from the far-left hand side with another shirt button ready to use, but that would have been a waste of her special sleeping gas for he was already unconscious.

After putting the button back in her pocket, the Clandestine Crusader removed the man's belt and used it to secure his hands behind his back.

A quick search only revealed a wallet with several hundred dollars in various American denominations and a Florida driver's license, which Solitaire took a quick cellphone photo of before returning it.

With his wallet back in place she looked around the room. The missing buttons took longer to find, but his cellphone was within a foot of where it fell when the fight started.

It was a basic model. No photos were in its memory and the phone had no apps beyond what the manufacturer installed. She checked the directory, but there was only the same number listed in both Recent History and Contacts. *One burner phone calling another burner?* Solitaire knew how difficult the disposable devices were to trace but would still make the attempt later.

The clipboard took a beating. Its bottom was now noticeably dented in the middle and would no longer lay upon a totally flat surface. Yet that side could be hidden from view easily enough, for she still had to confirm Fredrick Andrews status.

CHAPTER 22

With the suspect prepared for eventual discovery, Solitaire paused at the waiting room door and turned the knob. When it would move no further, she slowly pulled it fully open before quickly stepping outside. In the hallway once more as the door silently closed behind her, she was thankful that the guard wasn't looking in her direction at that moment, although she had a plausible explanation ready if asked.

The doctor moved back toward the Nurses' Station while pretending to fill out another form within the clipboard. A quick glance confirmed the real doctor was still inside the break room, enjoying something to eat.

A lot of potential scenarios had crossed her mind for getting a confirmation glance at Fredrick Andrews, but none which would not cause a commotion or put Solitaire in potential danger.

She was about to resume standing at the end of the counter out of everyone's way and bide her time when a nurse walked by, carrying a small tray that held a tiny paper cup of pills and a miniature bottle of water.

Solitaire expected the woman to turn either left or right at the intersection, but the hospital employee stopped directly before the guard in front of Andrews' door.

"It's time for the patient's medications," the nurse explained to the sentry, presenting the tray for his inspection.

Solitaire changed course and headed back toward the main hallway as the guard allowed the nurse inside. He didn't think twice about a doctor approaching his position, especially when the physician turned to the right and entered the patient's room diagonally across from him.

When his eyes went from right to left to complete the current surveillance sweep of the area, the guard saw the doctor standing at the foot of the sleeping patient's bed, glancing at the various monitor readings while making notes on something in a clipboard.

The sentry didn't know that Solitaire was just pantomiming being a concerned physician as she discretely kept an eye on the door behind him.

When it started to open, the doctor's departure was timed to have a clear line of sight across the hall and into the room being guarded as the nurse left.

There was Fredrick Andrews, lying on his bed staring at the ceiling. He was wearing a neck brace and a short-sleeved hospital gown, as evident by his arms resting above the bed blanket because of the IV feed connected to the left.

With the mission accomplished, the doctor kept walking down the corridor toward the elevator at the far end.

I hate leaving an assignment unfinished, but the authorities should be capable of making sure Andrews gets home alright this time, Solitaire thought while summoning the elevator.

Unfortunately, the car did not arrive empty.

As the doors opened, a hospital security guard appeared.

Solitaire had yet to encounter this one in any disguise, so she casually walked past him to enter the elevator as he exited.

The uniformed man eyed the doctor carefully before saying, "Where's your name tag?"

"Huh?" the faux doctor replied, acting surprised at the question while looking at where it should be pinned. "I told them earlier the clasp was cracked. Must have fallen off somewhere," Solitaire answered, trying not to look suspicious while pushing the Door Close button to expedite the process.

"I know we've been busy, but that's no excuse for us dropping the ball," the guard complained. "I'll radio ahead for you. Stop by the Security Office and someone will meet you there to fix the problem."

"Okay. Thanks," the disguised doctor said as the elevator doors closed.

Even if he doesn't find my parting gift right away, I better get out of here, thought Solitaire as she pushed the button for each of the lower four floors.

+++

"Where's your name tag?"

After finishing his radio call, the security guard gave the police officer standing in front of the room further down the hall a brief nod of acknowledgment. Then he began his rounds by peering into the waiting room.

While not unusual to see someone anxious for word of a patient's condition even at such a late hour, the guard was shocked to discover how the lone person within was arranged. The man was kneeling with his head on the seat cushion below a bad crack in the wall. Hands tied behind him by what appeared to be his own belt.

The guard entered and summoned backup over his radio as he checked for a pulse. Then he went back outside long enough to request medical assistance.

The floor doctor on duty came straight from the break room and began examining the unexpected patient while the guard paused to scan the note sitting in the next chair, laying on top of a bouquet of flowers.

It read in small, nondescript block letters: "Possible concussion. Definitely involved in the plot against Fredrick Andrews. Normally we don't operate within the United States but with a traitorous Consulate Agent involved, wanted to make sure subject was okay."

As the icing on the cake for her gift to law enforcement, Solitaire had signed the note "Concerned Intelligence Agent," to throw any investigations off her trail.

+++

As the elevator doors closed, Solitaire pushed the button for each of the lower floors but got off at the next stop. Except for patient rooms being semi-private, the fourth's layout was similar to the fifth's, allowing her direct access to the waiting room across the hall.

Although a doctor entered, it was a nurse who emerged a couple of moments later, for Solitaire hastily removed and donned over her clothing one of the teal scrubs sets from inside her shirt that caused the illusion of being somewhat overweight.

Her cheeks' cotton wadding went in the trash while everything else was wrapped within the doctor's jacket and shoved under a chair to delay their eventual discovery. Now visually a new person, Solitaire summoned the elevator again.

Alone in the car during its direct journey to the ground floor, after a quick phone call she took a selfie of herself before opening what the icon claimed was an e-copy of *The Count of Monte Cristo* by Alexandre Dumas. The symbol actually hid remote access to Solitaire's computerized alias generator, which matched the photo and other data she hastily keyed in against possible alternate identities.

When the elevator doors opened, off-duty nurse Lisa Hoyt casually exited and walked out of the hospital to patiently wait until the taxi she requested arrived.

+++

Nurse Hoyt had the cab take her to another hospital because their destination was allegedly short staffed and needed help. After using her cellphone to electronically pay the fare from a dummy account, Solitaire waited until the taxi was out of sight before walking away from the building as if just getting off work.

At the first opportunity she digitally switched personas again and threw the scrubs under a trash can where hopefully someone in need would find them.

Back in Alistair Burke's attire but now using a different alias, she called for another cab to continue her journey. It would be well into the morning before Solitaire safely reached the Miami sanctuary where she could rest and plan her next move but, other than needing to find a way to physically have alternate credentials available when necessary, thought this mission had gone well so far.

+++

Twenty-four hours later, the first hints of a new dawn were barely visible in the Eastern sky as an average looking panel van parked within the gray recesses of a Miami back alley.

In its rear, the Anbessas' technical expert Alberto Aguilar announced, "It's ready," after pushing a few more buttons on a modified laptop computer.

With that, another man opened the van's side panel door just enough for the XDS-1 to leave.

The stolen Andrews Aviation drone silently took to the skies as its sensors began their electronic search.

When its initial inquiry yielded no results, the unit undertook a wider circular flight pattern while maintaining the van as its focal point. Air samples were continuously collected and analyzed. Allowing for current wind direction and speed, the drone altered course appropriately with the results of each test.

Within a couple of minutes its objective was achieved as the XDS-1 hovered quietly over a seemingly abandoned warehouse. Altitude was gradually decreased until its camera had clear focus upon the view through a skylight without the armed guards stationed across the rooftop aware that they had been discovered.

"We have something," Aguilar reported, looking at the video feed the drone sent back. After confirming the unit's location, he rapidly enlarged a city map for all within the van to view on the computer screen.

"Damn. It's deeper within their territory than I suspected," César Fernandez said from the front passenger seat, in regard to where the red dot was placed.

"Orders?" someone else in the back asked, while checking their weapon.

"I know we can take them, but perhaps there's a better way," their leader replied, pulling out his cellphone to make a call.

"H-hello?" a groggy male voice answered on the other end.

"Hola and good morning mi amigo. You know who this is."

"Yes, I do, but I... requested that you never call me at home. If my wife were here..." the man said nervously.

"We both know she is still out of town with your daughter visiting her mother right now. I hope the Señorita you requested has been all you expected her to be," César said politely.

"The lady's asleep next to me at the moment, but she was everything you promised, and more," he added, pausing to look at the naked black-haired beauty lying next to him. "I assume it's time for me to return your... favor?"

"Si. It's time to take care of the Royales. They've been interfering with my business long enough," César complained.

"I agree that gang is a problem but as I've said before, even if I knew where their factory was, I still need probable cause to proceed."

"I can give you both their location and the excuse to raid it within seconds," the caller claimed, while pointing to Aguilar with his free hand.

The man in bed heard his cellphone ping and looked to see a text had just arrived.

"I would appreciate them dealt with by noon," César requested.

"You couldn't wait until after... breakfast?" the man on the other end asked, torn between the sleeping Señorita and looking at what he was sent.

"Now, now. Business before pleasure," César said with a chuckle.

"Is this accurate, let alone legally obtained?"

"Take care of them before noon and you can have Juanita again for another night on the house, mi capitán," César promised, ignoring the questions. "Otherwise..."

"I'll honor my end," the man said, before abruptly ending the call.

The men in the van saw a smile form on their leader's face as he put his cellphone away. "Whoever said the police can be unfriendly and uncooperative just didn't know how to handle them. Soon the Royales will be nothing but a bad memory as the Anbessas move up in the world," he proclaimed.

CHAPTER 23

Upon her safe arrival, Solitaire paused long enough to initiate a data search on her waiting room sparring partner before going to bed.

Yet less than two hours later, her slumber was disturbed by a beeping noise.

I didn't set a wake up call and that's not any of the emergency alarms, she realized, knowing that her Miami sanctuary remained secured.

She walked into the next room and discovered that the computer program which screened every petition for assistance had flagged a priority request.

This goes even deeper than I first suspected, Solitaire realized upon seeing who needed help.

+++

Carol Evans thought it odd that Ariel Andrews never left her office since letting everyone return to work from their involuntary time off. While long hours figuratively chained to a desk was just part of business, the personal assistant somehow still needed to make sure Andrews suspected the prearranged patsy, and not her, of being the company traitor.

Yet there were other tasks to do besides her lover's she thought as she pushed the intercom button.

"What is it, Carol?"

"Sorry for the intrusion. There's a Ms. Iris Higgins here from Hudson Electronics who claims to have a 2:30 appointment with you. Yet for some reason I have no record of it."

"Because I made it yesterday while you were away," Andrews replied. "Send her in."

Carol watched the visitor in a light gray but feminine cut business suit stride confidently into Andrews' office, glad to be rid of the chatty sales representative who never stopped talking except when she was on the intercom. Yet Evans never suspected that the visitor locked the door behind her.

Alone in the outer office again, a quick Internet search via her computer confirmed that Hudson Electronics was a young but rising start up on the West Coast with no relation to the similarly named company in the United Kingdom. *Now why would Andrews want to deal with someone like them,* she wondered, not knowing that the website had only been in existence for just over an hour.

Yet Carol had a way to find out as she removed a wireless earbud from her desk drawer.

+++

"Hello Ms. Andrews and thank you for allowing me a brief moment out of your busy schedule," the new arrival said upon entering as the CEO rose to greet her.

Ariel couldn't help noticing that Higgins was her height, but the eyes and hair were both brown, compared to her own blue and natural blonde, as she was handed a business card. However, instead of the normal contact information one would expect to find, it said in small block letters: PLEASE PRETEND THIS IS A NORMAL BUSINESS MEETING UNTIL I SAY OTHERWISE.

Ariel nodded in agreement as Higgins set her briefcase down in one of the guest chairs facing Andrews' desk and pulled her cellphone out from a jacket pocket. Yet instead of summoning some type of video presentation, Iris pushed a couple of icons on the screen before she slowly started walking around the room with it.

As Higgins began talking about what Hudson Electronics could do for Andrews Aviation, Ariel realized the other woman was scanning her office for any listening devices.

Ariel stood by the front corner of the desk and listened to the recital, noting that Iris never missed a beat in her presentation while continuing the electronic search. She went along with the act and asked an occasional question as if this were a real business meeting while Higgins worked her way to the entrance down one side of the office before starting back along the opposing wall.

Andrews watched Higgins move the phone slowly over every conceivable inch of office space before returning to scan her desk from one side to the other. The executive admired the lady's attention to detail, but everything seemed as it should be until the visitor reached the intercom.

While still reciting her sales presentation Higgins picked it up, nodded, then turned the device so Andrews could see that attached to its bottom by some sort of adhesive was a disc shaped object the same size as the top of a pencil's unused eraser.

Iris could see the look of shock on Ariel's face, but shook her head to keep Andrews silent.

Higgins continued talking while putting her cellphone down. Then she pulled out of another jacket pocket what looked like a metal rectangle much smaller than a travel size package of tissues.

Iris placed the object on the desk then slid its top open before peeling the listening device off the intercom and sticking it inside.

After sliding the box shut again, Higgins stopped her recital and revealed "There's a small but powerful magnet inside the container. The bug is getting fricasseed now and will be examined later to determine where it came from and who left it."

"I thank you for finding that damn thing, but I know the answer to the latter," Andrews began. "Yet how do I know you're the person I'm expecting?"

"Cautious. I like that. Alone and adrift in a sea of trouble?" the disguised Solitaire asked, before reciting her website's entire opening message.

+++

Iris Higgins was more energetic than most sales people, but what Carol Evans heard over her ear bud was all pretty much routine.

She listened to Ariel's standard recounting that Andrews Aviation was founded by a distant ancestor shortly after witnessing the Wright Brothers' historic flight at Kitty Hawk, North Carolina; with the corporate headquarters eventually relocated from there to Miami during the opening days of the Space Race because real estate was tight close to Cape Canaveral.

Bored, Evans was about to put everything away when the conversation suddenly stopped in mid-sentence.

At first she thought there might be something wrong with either her cellphone or the eavesdropping app, but a quick check showed everything appeared fine on her end. Going back to replay the last few seconds proved even the recording abruptly ended at the same point.

Nothing during the meeting indicated something was wrong with the illegal listening device, *Yet I can't check it out until after Andrews leaves and I have a chance to sneak in there. Whatever is going on, I better let César know.*

+++

As the ladies sat down to have their real meeting, Andrews revealed, "I got your contact information from my parents, after they used your company to rescue my brother in Cancun."

"How is Fredrick?" Solitaire asked, occupying the chair next to the one with her briefcase.

"Still a bit shaken up, but no long term physical injuries," replied Ariel. "A joint police and FBI team escorted him home last night."

"Good. We had some… interesting times getting him back to the states," Solitaire said, still acting like a whole team was involved instead of just her.

"My father said he used your services once long before the Cancun incident but, while I'll pay whatever it takes to resolve this matter, truthfully I've never heard of your agency," added Andrews.

Her guest only nodded, knowing it must have been a previous Solitaire in that matter. "I'm not surprised," she began. "It may not be the best business model for a commercial enterprise, but we depend strictly upon word of mouth and live on our good reputation. That way we can stay low profile but highly dependable. Although it isn't written with the periods, Solitaire is an acronym. Depending upon the situation, our agency can provide Security Officers, Licensed Investigators, Technical Advisors, Insurance Representation and Everything else you might need to legally address any problem you haven't been able to find a solution to," was her rehearsed but inaccurate response. "And don't worry. We can work something out later," she promised, knowing those in need were never charged any fee for services rendered since the Daye Foundation secretly underwrote the entire Solitaire operation.

"Between my brother and the drone, it's obvious that someone is targeting us," began Ariel, before recounting the theft of the XDS-1.

When Andrews finished, Solitaire picked up her cellphone and said, "A drug sniffing drone can be a marvelous thing in the right hands. Yet it does have other potential applications. I saw this on the news while preparing to come here," she added, after calling up a headline.

"Local gang's drug factory raided," Ariel read, before scanning the article. "That does sound like our drone," she confirmed, handing back the phone.

"The local precinct captain would only say the tip came from a verifiable but confidential informant. The fact that the police confiscated over a hundred pounds of meth, cocaine and who knows what else speaks volumes towards your device's capabilities. Yet some other gang now has less competition to worry about," the Clandestine Crusader pointed out.

"True," agreed Andrews. "With the XDS-1, they could certainly wipe out their enemies and corner the market in no time. Yet that isn't what made me suspicious of something being wrong in Andrews Aviation to begin with."

"Oh?"

"While I'm not directly involved in every minute detail of the company's daily workings, I am hands on as much as my schedule permits," explained Ariel. "Over the past year, I've began noticing discrepancies in shipping invoices between us and various clients across Mexico, along with Central and

South America. Our records would show X amount of weight in mostly parts going to the airlines and government air forces that America is friendly with, yet copies of the delivery receipts we receive later showed higher amounts arriving at their destinations than what we originally shipped."

"And this is only on exporting, not imports?"

"Yes. When it happens, there's always extra items listed passing through customs than what Andrews Aviation originally packed. Our clients are never charged for the additional materials. Yet while we're not short any inventory, we do have to pay the extra shipping fees and duties for whatever is sent on the increased orders. That's why I privately asked Fredrick to go down there in the first place. He discretely checked out a few destinations and discovered no one could account for the surplus parts and equipment they allegedly got, because somehow everything disappeared from their warehouses within days of its arrival. Yet since they were never billed for the additional materials, no one down there ever bothered to raise a fuss, thinking it was just clerical errors on our part. An occasional mistake, maybe. But continually for over a year?"

"I see..." said Solitaire. "If the discrepancies were inbound, my first thought would be someone is using your company as a cover to smuggle in drugs. Yet exporting makes me think ghost guns."

"Ghost guns?" repeated Andrews, not recognizing the term.

"It's a generic name for any homemade firearm. Nowadays any individual with the right equipment can make the parts to assemble a weapon in their own home. Some are even using computer programs and 3D printers to avoid metal detectors."

"They can even make the ammunition?"

"In time, but you have to be more cautious with the ingredients involved," Solitaire pointed out. "The reason for the name is because the finished fire arms have no manufacturer serial numbers, let alone registrations. The problem is bad enough here in the United States. Imagine a more organized operation mass producing parts and smuggling them to be assembled and used in places where every official weapon must be registered with and accounted for by the local authorities, who enforce limitations on how many each person can have in hopes of curtailing violent situations."

Ariel nodded. "The local gangs and cartels down there must have a field day with them."

"Yes, with whoever is behind it all raking in top dollar and the authorities none the wiser until they come across one. Probably at a crime scene."

"Damn. And I sent Fredrick—"

"Not your fault. The kidnapping, while related, is part of a bigger agenda someone has against your family," Solitaire said.

"While competition can be fierce at times, especially over the last decade or so, it's never gotten to the point of–"

"Could the problem be personal instead of professional?"

"How?" Ariel asked in return. "Dad always stressed honesty and integrity, whether dealing with a customer, a supplier or an employee. While I've only been in charge since he retired two years ago because of his health, I know of no enemies—professional or personal—who would stoop so low."

Considering what was necessary to even briefly portray Reginald Andrews... Solitaire was lost in thought until Ariel asked what her agency's course of action would be.

"First I'll need a list of everyone who works in Shipping and Receiving."

"Already prepared," replied Andrews, reaching under her desk blotter to pull out a folder with the requested information.

Handing it to the woman she only knew as Iris Higgins, Ariel added, "Everyone passed a background check as part of being considered for employment."

Solitaire nodded as she looked over the list. "We'll be rerunning them again, just in case because I already see one red flag. This man here was arrested at the hospital where your brother was after trying to check out the security arrangements there," she revealed, while pointing to one specific name.

Andrews cursed a short string of expletives, ending with "I'm gonna fire Carol."

"Carol Evans? Your personal assistant? Why do you suspect her?"

"Besides being the only person other than myself with the security clearances needed to obtain the propitiatory information necessary to pull off the drone theft as smoothly as it happened, she can also go to Shipping and Receiving or anywhere else across the complex without anyone giving her a second thought. She handles a lot of the daily paperwork too, including reviewing invoices, before my final approval and is also the only one who could have planted that bug in my office."

"No cleaning staff?" Solitaire asked in disbelief.

"Not in here," Andrews replied. "I don't ask anyone to do anything I can do for myself, so I do my own cleaning. Partly for security reasons and partly because I'm somewhat of a neat freak."

"I can see that," Solitaire said, noting how pristine the office looked, with no indication that Ariel Andrews had confined herself to it during her private investigation. "How is security at your private residence?"

"I live in a gated apartment complex in town. My folks and Fredrick are still in the family home on the outskirts of the city. Security is tight at both. You'd need an army to get into either one."

Or a Trojan Horse, realized Solitaire. "Okay. Here's what we're going to do," she said, while reaching for her briefcase.

+++

César Fernandez was enjoying a private victory celebration when his cellphone rang.

He had hoped it was just Carol calling to congratulate him, for they had plans to meet again later that evening, but wasn't happy to hear the topic of conversation.

"I admit it could be a technical issue, but until you can check it out..." he began, as a hand gently started to caress his bare back.

"Si. We can definitely advance our timetable if necessary, but confirm what happened first if you can. I'll talk to you later," César promised, ending the call just as the hand went someplace it shouldn't have while he was on the phone.

After the device was back on his dresser, César complained, "You loco chica," while turning over in bed to face the lady with him. "Never do that while I'm discussing important business."

"Am I not important too?" Juanita wanted to know.

"Si, but for different reasons," César conceded before kissing her.

When their lips parted, Juanita asked "Do I have to go back to that captain tonight? He is nothing but a mangy alley cat compared to the Anbessas."

"True," César agreed, holding her naked body closer to his, "but he was loyal and loyalty must be rewarded."

"And my loyalty to you?" she asked slyly, while brushing her fingertips against his chest.

"It shall be rewarded also," César promised. *But if you ever displease me...* was the unspoken thought as he began kissing his way down her neck.

CHAPTER 24

Carol Evans was back at her desk working after the clandestine restroom call when Iris Higgins left—a lot more silently than when the chatty sales lady arrived. Evans' just smiled behind the lady's back, figuring the appointment didn't go well.

About a half hour later Ariel Andrews appeared in the doorway between outer and inner offices just long enough to let Carol know she would be working late again, but the personal assistant could leave whenever she wished since it was after five.

Evans was happy to hear this, for it meant rendezvousing with her boyfriend sooner than expected.

Yet, while she wasn't sure what, something seemed… off about Andrews. Was all the stress finally taking its toll?

"Is everything all right?" Carol asked, wondering what it was that made her take a second look at her employer. Except for maybe a hint of dark circles under the eyes, Andrews looked okay physically.

Ariel paused before replying. "I know who the traitor within the company is. Still haven't figured out yet if he has any accomplices or why the XDS-1 was stolen, let alone what their ultimate goal might be."

Carol knew Andrews using the male pronoun meant she was going after the patsy! "I can stay late if you need—"

"That's okay. You have a good night and I'll see you tomorrow." With that Andrews went back into her private office, locking the door behind her.

Damn. I won't be able to check on the bug until sometime tomorrow at the earliest. But at least I know she's on the "right" track, was Evans' happy thought as she shut down her computer and prepared to leave.

+++

Despite wishing her night with César could have lasted longer and blissfully unaware of his afternoon tryst with Juanita, Evans was back at work bright and early the next morning.

It was well before eight when she pressed the intercom button on her desk, for no answer would mean an empty office and a golden opportunity to check the bug's status, but—

"Did you need anything Carol?" came the transmitted reply.

What the hell did Andrews do? Spend the night in there again? Evans silently wondered. *She must have no social life at all.* "Just wanted to let you know I'm here. Do you need—"

"If there is, I'll call," said Andrews, abruptly ending the conversation.

With that Carol went to work, hoping there would be an opportunity later while still thinking there was something 'off' about her legitimate employer.

The chance didn't arrive until almost eleven, when Ariel Andrews suddenly came out of her office and said, "I've got to go down to R and D. Hold my calls until I get back."

Evans just simply nodded as Andrews briskly walked past, wearing a sky blue but feminine cut business suit. *At least she changed clothes since yesterday.* The personal assistant waited a few minutes in case Ariel came back for something because she left with just her cellphone.

Upon feeling it safe to do so, Carol rose from her chair and went directly to the inner office, but was surprised to find the door locked. *She's never done that before during the day when it's just me out here.*

With a puzzled frown, Evans went back to her desk for the secretly made duplicate key from its hiding place she used whenever Andrews was away.

Once inside the executive's office she went straight to the intercom, but was shocked to discover the listening device gone.

I've got to warn César. We need to finish this now, was Carol's lone thought as she left the office after putting the device back in place.

Solitaire stared at her cellphone. The image transmitted from the hidden security camera in Andrews' office was very telling. *There's more than enough evidence to arrest the inside person now, but who is Carol Evans working for? And what will they do next?*

The answers came later that day.

The Chief Executive of Andrews Aviation left late as usual, but with just enough time to arrive at a local grocery store for some quick shopping before it closed.

Despite it being a week night, the almost full parking lot proved Ariel wasn't the only customer in need of food. The first available space was in the center, closer to the street than the store.

Tired, Ariel got out and clicked the key fob's lock button before setting the car alarm. She never bothered changing into something else. The gold necklace with its amethyst pendant, along with the matching ear rings, were a part of practically every outfit she wore.

With keys in her short purse, Ariel started toward the store when a black four door sedan came down the lane in such a manner that it looked to be intentionally blocking Andrews' path.

She was about to change direction, even walk between cars to another lane if necessary, when the parking lot lights suddenly disappeared as something was pulled over her head.

Andrews tried to fight back, but there was no escape. Within seconds both arms were secured as Ariel felt herself being dragged by an attacker on each side.

A hand over her mouth muffled any screams as she was roughly shoved into the idling vehicle that blocked her path.

The whole event occurred in a matter of seconds, with the car accelerating out of the parking lot before anyone nearby even considered possibly coming to Andrews' rescue.

+++

The terrifying artificial darkness had surrounded her for some time. Its stifling source not only made it difficult to breathe, but cut off all sensory input except for some hearing and feeling of motion. Other than knowing the difference between a left and right turn, Andrews couldn't say where they were headed but if asked, could guess why she was taken.

"Keys. Credit cards. Cellphone. Nice wad of cash," someone up front announced, obviously going through her purse.

"Don't forget this," a gruff voice on Ariel's left said as she felt her digital wristwatch being removed. For some reason they never took her earrings or necklace. She was still dressed, *but will that change when we reach our destination?*

Ariel Andrews felt frightened and alone, squeezed between two of her kidnappers in the back seat.

Her hands and feet remained untied, but she was far from free.

Blindly led around by her captors, she had no idea how much time passed before the vehicle stopped.

Ariel heard a door open, then was dragged out of the car and forcibly escorted up a couple of steps before involuntarily ascending a larger flight of stairs to the second floor of their unknown destination.

At the top of the landing she was hastily chaperoned and partially dragged like a child's toy, until a sudden stop heralded the hood being removed.

"Make yourself comfortable. You're going to be here awhile," revealed one of her kidnappers.

She found herself standing in the middle of a small room. Thick wall to wall carpeting covered the floor. The walls were a dull, off white color.

Andrews turned and demanded to know, "Why have you kidnapped me?"

"Kidnap is such a harsh word," another man replied. He was at least six feet tall with neatly groomed black hair but, unlike the others, was clean shaven. "Let us say you are my guest."

The kidnappers' apparent leader was far better dressed and acted more civilized than the other two, who kept watching her.

They made Ariel uneasy. Like they had other things on their mind than ransom, so she asked, "Then I'm free to leave?" walking toward the better dressed one and the exit.

"Sure," the man said with a smile. "After I get what I want," he added in a more menacing tone, before forcibly shoving her away from the door.

Caught off guard, Andrews staggered backward a couple of steps before losing her balance. She fell and landed on the carpet rump first.

This made all her captors laugh.

"You can't do this to me!" Ariel protested, while trying to get up. "I'm—"

"Save the spiel. I know who I'm dealing with," the leader replied. "Ariel Andrews, only daughter of Reginald and Sarah Andrews. You're a divorced workaholic in her late twenties with no kids. Maybe a few friends but no one who will miss you before our business is concluded, and if it isn't to my satisfaction..." The man emphasized those last words by taking the index finger of one hand and dragging it across his throat.

Speechless, Ariel just stood and stared angrily at him as the kidnappers left the room, locking the door behind them.

She noted there was no doorknob on her side, meaning only whoever was outside controlled access. *Just like a prison cell.*

The leader's comments did have her concerned. The Andrews family had plenty of resources both private and professional if this was just another ransom attempt. *Yet why did they keep Fredrick after getting the money?*

With nothing else to do, Ariel started searching her surroundings.

There were two other doors besides the entrance. Behind the first was a private bathroom with only what one would expect to find, including soap, towels and toilet paper. The medicine cabinet over the basin was completely empty. Even the shelves had been removed. Its counterpart below the sink held only pipes. The fixtures and walls matched the outer room décor. Even the grout and tile around the bathtub were the same dull shade.

There was no closet. Worse, despite the fact the room had an active overhead light fixture and outlets for electricity and other utilities, there was no phone or television, let alone anything that could access the Internet. While her briefcase was still locked in the car until the kidnappers decided otherwise, Ariel didn't know where the rest of her stuff was.

The only piece of furniture in this prison was a full size bed in one corner.

Searching the rest of the 'accommodations' found nothing that might aid an escape attempt. Andrews did take some satisfaction in confirming that there were no cameras, meaning no interior surveillance.

The second door was sliding glass. A privacy curtain obscured viewing it in full but opening that revealed metal fencing across the exterior instead of a traditional screen, keeping anyone without the key inside. The balcony outside ran the length of the door, but its width was only a step or two at most from the attached barrier.

The glass fixture was the room's sole access for natural light and only air

...the room's sole access to natural light...

source other than a heating duct. Seeing no sign of any alarms or other booby traps, Andrews cautiously unlocked and opened the door for some fresh air.

After a quick shake of the gate confirmed it was secure, she looked through the fencing's metal bars at her surroundings, thanks to the building's exterior lighting.

The well-maintained grounds appeared broken on either side of the small balcony by a decorative garden walkway, giving the impression of viewing somebody's backyard. Ariel had no clue what might be underneath or above her but ahead was a wide lawn before a line of tall trees, guaranteeing privacy from whatever might be on the natural curtain's other side.

Yet even if she could get outside, the armed guards on patrol were another matter.

There were currently two, routinely walking toward each other before turning to go back wherever they came from. Each muscle-bound man looked like they lived in a gym when not on duty, for they appeared capable of bench pressing a car single hand when not carrying some kind of rifle like it was a prized possession. Neither wore any kind of uniform, which meant they were personally employed by whoever was holding her.

Even if the known obstacles could be overcome, what laid beyond the trees that might impede an escape attempt?

Leaving the glass door open for some fresh air in case they attempted to send something harmful through the ventilation vent, Ariel Andrews sat on the edge of the bed to contemplate her future.

+++

César Fernandez nodded to the man he left posted outside his captive's locked door, then walked down the hallway to another bedroom.

"So?" Carol Evans asked, rising up from her lover's bed wearing only a sexy lingerie outfit that wouldn't be on much longer.

"¡Magnífico!" he exclaimed with a smile while starting to undress. "By this time tomorrow I shall have reclaimed everything the Andrews family ever stole from me, leaving them poorer than the lowest homeless person in the world!"

"¡Buena!" Carol happily replied, seductively licking her lips as she approached him. *I shall have all I want soon too, and after that...* was her last thought as they kissed.

CHAPTER 25

A sharp knock upon the wooden door disturbed what little sleep Ariel Andrews had managed to get. The only clue concerning time was a hint of daylight shining through the glass door. She would never publicly admit to feeling tired but vowed to overcome whatever lay ahead.

Andrews just lay there, staring at the ceiling that matched the rest of her prison as the sound of a key being inserted within the door lock meant impending company. Her captors or their leader would eventually reveal what they wanted, but she was surprised to hear a woman's voice say "Señorita?"

Ariel only turned her head to look at the new arrival, a Hispanic lady about her age wearing a formal maid's uniform. "What would you like to eat?" the servant asked, as casually as a waitress in any restaurant. If the maid had any sympathy for Andrews' plight, she never showed it.

"I'm not hungry," Ariel replied, rotating in bed so her back was to the maid.

"I shall let my employer know."

Andrews didn't care if the lady stayed or left but drew little satisfaction from hearing someone relock the door. She liked the next intrusion of her cell a few minutes later even less.

"What's this about you not being hungry? We've got a big day ahead and it's not right to face it on an empty stomach."

Ariel recognized the head kidnapper's voice. "Like I told your maid. Unless I get to go somewhere I want to be, I'm not hungry," she replied, curious about what he had planned but not bothering to turn around and look at him.

"Have it your way, but it's time for you to earn your keep," was his cold reply.

"What do you mean?" Andrews wondered, raising her head just long enough to see that the man was wearing a different suit than yesterday's and carried a garment bag that looked familiar.

His response was to toss the bag onto the bed at Ariel's bare feet, for her shoes were the only thing the woman bothered removing before laying down last night.

"I took the liberty of choosing an outfit for you, but you really should consider buying more attractive clothing. With your looks and figure…" he began as she sat up.

Upon unzipping the bag enough to see what was within, blue eyes widened in shock as Andrews realized, "You've been in my condo!"

"What's the old saying? In for a penny, in for a pound?" the leader asked, leaning against the wall by the bathroom door so he could keep an eye on her.

"Entering it European style was a nice touch, but you really should pick a more complicated pass code for that security system than your birth date, although you don't look your age."

Andrews couldn't help wondering how he figured out the code. *Someone connected with the security company?* Yet, other than staring at him angrily, Ariel had no response except to ask what he wanted from her.

"Like I said, we've a big day ahead of us," the man repeated. "Be ready to go in an hour," he added, leaving the 'Or else' unspoken but implied.

With that the leader left the room, the door being locked afterward.

Ariel stared at the barrier to her freedom long after his departure, then reluctantly got out of bed and answered nature's call.

After washing her hands, she looked at herself in the bathroom mirror. Dark circles appeared under blue eyes from lack of sleep. Ariel knew her breath smelled from not getting to brush her teeth last night, but otherwise she was fine at the moment.

Her stomach gurgled in complaint of its emptiness, yet Andrews knew not to eat any food her captors offered in case it was laced with something.

She had spent hours examining every nook and cranny of the small bedroom prison in hope of finding even a slim opportunity for escape, but sadly none arose.

At one point breaking the bathroom mirror to obtain a makeshift weapon was considered, but even with a towel to attempt protecting them, the risk to her hands was too great.

Despite knowing she was not being monitored, Ariel refused to risk taking a shower and instead freshened up the best she could at the basin before reluctantly donning the other outfit. It was another of the many feminine business suits she owned, but the design was more stylish for presentations and meetings. Her captor didn't think to bring any shoes, and she wasn't willing to part with her birthstone jewelry.

As prepared as she could be, Ariel Andrews laid back down and awaited whatever fate might lie ahead.

+++

Andrews could only guess that an hour had passed when the head kidnapper returned. Yet she was shocked to see who was with him.

"YOU! You're so fired you—" she started yelling at Carol Evans, leaping off the bed in anger to physically attack the traitorous personal assistant.

"You will not talk to my woman that way," the leader warned Andrews, as he punched her in the stomach.

Ariel took a step back, doubling over in pain as Carol smiled.

"Be thankful that I cannot risk doing anything that will leave a visible mark before your part in what is about to happen is over but be warned. I do not tolerate insubordination from anyone. If you push me too far, you *will* suffer the consequences!" Evans' boyfriend said angrily.

"And what do you hope will happen today?" Andrews wondered while straightening back up again.

"Today is the day I fully reclaim everything that should be rightfully mine," he boasted. "You will take me to see your father and we will settle our differences man to man."

"But he hasn't seen anyone since—"

"I don't care. He *will* see me!"

"And if I refuse?" Ariel asked.

"There are many ways a person can be hurt before dying," he replied while pulling out a .45 caliber gun from the shoulder holster hidden under his jacket. "I can either see your father today, or I can see him at your funeral."

+++

Ariel Andrews' departure was her arrival in reverse. The sight concealing hood was placed upon her head before being escorted out of the makeshift prison.

She felt again the same sensations of someone on each side taking her down a long flight of stairs. Then through a door and descending a couple of more steps before being shoved into the back seat of a car.

Once they were well underway, to Ariel's surprise the hood was removed. As her eyes adjusted to the sudden return of light, she saw things were different this time. Carol Evans sat next to the driver in the front seat. Last time the voice indicated it was another man in her place.

Only the leader was with Andrews in the back seat, sitting on her right. There was a black leather briefcase on the floor, cradled between his legs.

Of more importance was the gun he brandished earlier. It was lying on his lap. The man's right hand casually rested on top of it, but he could still grab and fire the weapon within seconds. That the muzzle was pointed at her abdomen wasn't lost on Ariel, so there would be no attempt to dash out the other door the moment the car had to stop at an intersection or make any other escape effort.

"No funny moves or I will pull the trigger," he warned her. "And trust me. Even if you get medical treatment in time, gut shots hurt like hell."

Andrews just nodded and tried to get comfortable. *I've got to be careful,* she realized. *The way he keeps changing his position about hurting me shows he's on edge as it is.*

She turned and watched the scenery pass by, the landmarks growing more familiar as the journey continued.

Although today was vastly different, it was a trip Ariel made on a regular basis and usually looked forward to.

She was headed home.

CHAPTER 26

"Look. Whatever it is you want or hope to achieve, can't I get it for you? There's no need to bother my folks. Especially my father," Ariel Andrews asked once more. Every previous attempt during their journey had fallen upon deaf ears, but hopefully this time...

"This is between your father and me, and I'm going to settle it once and for all," the man next to her replied, without even bothering to look at his prisoner.

"Why? What did he do?" Ariel got no answer.

Not knowing what else she could do at the moment, Ariel bent her head and brought both hands together under her chin to pray. The man beside her didn't say anything and the two up front were looking forward as Carol gave the driver directions, so no one noticed Ariel remove a disc smaller than a dime in circumference from the back of her amethyst pendant and secret it in her left hand.

As the sedan left the highway service road and turned onto the private lane that led to the Andrews estate, César Fernandez moved the gun from his lap to hide it between himself and the car door.

But that didn't lessen its threat.

"Remember to do your part right," he warned her in a low voice. "From this angle, I could easily shoot you in the spine and paralyze you for the rest of your miserable life."

"Why do you hate me so?" Ariel asked as the car approached the guard station before the entry gate.

"You specifically? No personal reason. Your family in general? Especially your father? That's another matter."

"Which you still won't tell me," Ariel complained, but there was no time for him to reply even if he wanted to as the car slowed to a stop with the engine idling. Its rear doors were even with the guard station sitting on its raised median between the entry and departure lanes. The driver lowered the left passenger window remotely as Ariel noticed the man next to her stare intently at his prisoner.

"Welcome back Miss Andrews. Nice to see you again," the uniformed security guard politely said, looking down into the vehicle from his booth position. "Although it's been quite a while since she was here last, I recognize Miss Evans but not the two gentlemen with you."

"One of the family lawyers," Ariel said, pointing to the man on her right, "and our driver," she added, indicating the other. "We have legal business to discuss with Dad."

"Okay. Go right on through," the guard replied, while pushing a button inside the booth.

Slowly, the iron gate pulled back to allow the car onto the fence-surrounded grounds.

Once the gate closed and the vehicle was no longer in sight, the guard reached for his cellphone.

"So far, so good," Carol Evans noted.

"The tough part is still ahead," her boyfriend answered, as their ride pulled up to and stopped at the front porch of a two-story structure that looked more like a miniature mansion than the large lavish house it was.

Ariel started to exit her door. With her body blocking anyone's view, the left hand managed to hide the disc in the crack between seat cushion and backrest when she was admonished "Out my side, and act like you would on any other visit here," César warned as he put the gun back in its shoulder holster.

With briefcase in hand he stepped out, then held the door open for Andrews.

Ariel scooted over to exit from his side and found herself immediately facing Evans. "My boyfriend isn't the only one armed," she warned Andrews, holding open her handbag long enough for Ariel to see the weapon within before it was quickly shut again.

"And why are you in on this?" Ariel wanted to know. The brief glance only confirmed Evans' handgun was a smaller caliber than his. Probably a 9mm with a standard magazine clip in the grip.

"If Little Miss Privileged hasn't figured that out by now, I don't have time to tell you," Carol said coldly. *Bet you didn't have to carry a mountain of student loan debt to earn your Masters of Business Administration degree!*

Meanwhile, César Fernandez stuck his head back inside the vehicle. "¿Sabes qué hacer?", wanting to make sure the driver knew his instructions.

"Si," the man answered, while placing an ear bud in his right ear so he could hear everything transmitted by the device his Jefe wore.

César stood erect again and saw Carol and Ariel glaring angrily at each other.

"When this is over," Evans threatened Andrews in a low voice.

"Bring it, if you dare," Ariel replied as he approached.

"Ladies," he said, more as a warning than an informal greeting. With that, Fernandez took a step back to let Ariel lead, but Carol was right behind her.

As the trio approached the rich mahogany front door, it was opened by the Major Domo of the household. "Miss Andrews, welcome home," he said in a proper British accent.

"Thank you, Abbott," replied Ariel.

"Miss Evans, It's been too long since you last graced us with your presence," the Major Domo added, formally greeting her.

"Couldn't be helped," was Carol's answer, while staring at Ariel again.

"Sir?" Abbott asked politely.

"I'm with Willowby and Associates," lied César. "We have some legal matters to discuss with Mister Andrews."

Ariel wasn't surprised Carol's accomplice knew the correct law firm, although it did earn Evans another quick angry glance that only Abbott didn't see.

"Reginald or Fredrick, sir?" the Major Domo asked.

"Both, if possible, but Reginald is the priority," César responded.

The Major Domo seemed to hesitate, but with a quick nod from Ariel, continued with his duties. "The master is in his study with Mrs. Sarah. Miss Ariel knows the way," Abbott replied, stepping aside to let the three of them enter. "I unfortunately do not know if Fredrick is in residence at the moment but if so, I shall endeavor to send him to you."

"This way," Ariel announced, trying to keep any emotion out of her voice.

She reluctantly led them across a marble foyer, past a staircase with well polished mahogany railings, to a matching wooden door on the other side.

With that, Ariel suddenly turned and faced her kidnappers. "Listen. I keep telling you that whatever it is you want, I'm sure something can be worked out just between the three of us," she pleaded. "There's no need to bother—"

"It's too late for negotiating," Carol answered, reaching past her to knock on the door.

There was a brief moment of silence before a female voice with a prominent British accent asked, "Who's there?"

Ariel just shook her head sadly and said, "It's me Mom. We need to see Dad."

"We?" Sarah Andrews repeated in surprise. "Ariel, you know your Father..."

Ariel turned her head, hoping she might still be able to persuade them to change plans, only to see César Fernandez briefly open his jacket just enough to remind her of the gun in its shoulder holster.

"I'm sorry Mom, but it couldn't be helped," Ariel said forlornly.

There was another, slightly longer pause, before Sarah said it was okay to enter the study.

Ariel opened the door and walked directly to her mother, who was standing near the entrance. The two women were the same height, but the Andrews matriarch was noticeably older. She wore a full-length long-sleeved dress. Her gray hair was tied up in a bun, giving anyone a clear view of the hearing aid in her left ear.

They hugged as Ariel whispered, "It's going to be okay."

Carol and César were only a second behind Ariel, but they stopped in mid-step upon fully being within the room. Whatever they might have expected to see versus the sight before them was two different things.

Most of the furniture one would expect to find in a study was gone. All that remained of the previous décor was one chair with a little credenza next to it in the room's far left-hand corner.

Reginald Fredrick Andrews occupied a slightly reclining position within a hospital style bed to the right of the original furniture, covered by a blanket from the shoulders down. Except for monitoring connections and an Intravenous feed on the left, his arms were bare below the short sleeves of sky-blue pajamas and rested on top of the royal blue fleece.

If not for the slow but steady movement of his chest, one would wonder about the man lying perfectly still within his oxygen tent. A collection of monitors showed his current health status.

Reginald's corner of the study was intentionally kept dark. If either of the new arrivals dared to take a closer look, they would see that except for his eyebrows and some patchy stubble from not shaving, the man had no hair. The fact that his facial skin tone looked ashen compared to the daylight coming through the windows on the far side of the room, along with the dark circles under his eyes, further confirmed the diagnosis that the patriarch of the Andrews clan was not a well man.

"Wh-what—" Evans started to say as she and César just stared at the man in the bed. While César had yet to meet him, this wasn't the Reginald Andrews Carol remembered. *What the hell is going on? He's still somewhat overweight, but much thinner than the last time I saw him. Granted, Reginald was always complaining about needing to lose weight, but the man was a lot more robust and outgoing than this.*

"Stage Four Pancreatic Cancer," began Ariel, answering what she assumed Carol's question to be. "It's why Dad retired two years ago. The new chemotherapy treatments his doctor wanted to try looked promising, but only bought him some time at best."

"Sadly, our physician doesn't give him more than another month or two at most," Sarah added, trying to keep her voice steady. "The only thing he wants in life now is to be with his family when…"

"I-I didn't know," Carol said, still staring at her former employer.

"No one outside of this household, except for medical personnel, knows," confirmed Mrs. Andrews.

"Of course you'd want to keep this private," realized Carol. "It's personal business, let alone the possible impact upon Andrews Aviation if word got out before Ariel made her mark in the industry. Yet if he had only kept his promise…"

"What promise?" inquired Ariel, but any response was interrupted by another outrage.

"I… After all these years, I will not be cheated out of my revenge!" César yelled, finding his voice again.

"What's he talking about?" mother asked daughter. No one noticed that the women had taken a protective position between the visitors and Reginald.

"Your family is about to return all that is rightfully mine," César proclaimed. "From ownership and control of what you call Andrews Aviation and the rest of everything you allegedly own, down to the last cent within your bank accounts."

"That's preposterous," replied Sarah as Ariel stared at her kidnapper in disbelief. "Why would you make such fantastical demands, let alone expect us to honor them?"

"Reginald Andrews refused to do the right thing, leaving my mother heartbroken and our family destitute. Now I will return the favor because I, César Hector Fernandez, intend to claim my true heritage and birthright as Reginald Andrews Junior!"

CHAPTER 27

The Andrews women were stunned to hear Fernandez's declaration, with the accused's wife the first to find her voice.

"How dare you!" Sarah began, while taking a step forward to confront the man. "My husband—"

"Cheated on you with my Madre long ago," repeated César. "I am the result of that betrayal. She said when your husband discovered he was to become a father, he refused to do the honorable thing, leaving the two of us abandoned for my entire life!"

"Preposterous!" declared Sarah. "My husband has been a great father to our two children."

"But Reginald Andrews has three," César countered. "From all the times she told it since I was old enough to understand, I know Beatriz Fernandez's story word for word. How, even though she was a native born American proud of her Hispanic heritage, the only jobs she could ever find were menial labor. She started out as a waitress, then a cook, before hooking up with a local employment service and assigned work as a maid for various clients, including your household.

"All the pictures of her younger self I've seen prove my mother was a beautiful lady even then, so it's no wonder that she caught your husband's attention," he continued. "Despite Reginald Andrews being married to you, in time they fell in love and stole secret, private moments with each other whenever you weren't around. Reginald swore he loved my mother with a passion that burned hotter than the sun, but the coward either couldn't or wouldn't find the courage to divorce you upon discovering her expecting."

"Sounds like a soap opera to me," commented Ariel.

"¡Silencio!" Fernandez yelled at her, before turning to face Sarah again. "All my Madre was ever able to give me was her name, the drive to succeed in life and a thirst for vengeance that must be sated! My only regret is that she didn't live to see this day."

"That your mother is no longer with us is the only thing you have my sympathy on, but I remember Beatriz Fernandez," admitted Sarah.

"Oh?" César was surprised to hear that.

"She wasn't a bad maid, but we had to fire both her and her boyfriend, our gardener Hector Jackson, for stealing from us," revealed Sarah.

"What?" said a shocked César.

"You can look up the court records for yourself if you don't believe me. Our lawyer said they served about six months in jail apiece since it was the first known offense for each but until now, I had no idea whatever happened to them after they were released."

"You're lying!" cursed César, his tone of voice growing angrier.

"No, I'm not," calmly replied Sarah Andrews. "Don't you get it? I have no idea why Beatriz would make up such outlandish stories but our old gardener from Chickpea, Alabama, your mother's boyfriend at the time, is your biological father. Not my husband César *Hector* Fernandez. You even look somewhat like him," she added.

"No!" yelled César in a louder voice while shaking his head in disbelief.

Carol Evans took a small step back from him, for she had never seen her boyfriend this angry before.

Thankfully César was so lost in his rage over being told the truth that he didn't notice.

"After *Reginald Andrews* abandoned us, my Madre had to do whatever she could to make ends meet and raise me," Fernandez claimed. "She toiled long hours day and night for weeks at a time with hardly a moment to herself but always made time to care for me. She insisted I stay in school and get good grades, but I still helped whenever I could. Somehow, we managed to survive, but there was never enough from one month to the next.

"As high school graduation approached, I knew I wanted more out of life than flipping burgers, trimming hedges or cleaning motel rooms like me Madre. Yet no matter how good your grades are, it still takes money to acquire an education beyond high school. Thankfully the Anbessas showed me the way, and I've gone from being just a lowly cub to leader of the pack.

"My courier had trouble delivering Fredrick his copies in Cancun," he said, addressing his captive audience again, "but I've had legal documents drawn up for each of you to sign over to me your share of the Andrews family fortune, as well as nullify all past, present or future claims to everything that should be rightfully mine," César added, while indicating the leather briefcase in his left hand.

"Not going to happen," Sarah calmly said.

"I am both Reginald's first and oldest son," Fernandez proclaimed, holding on to his delusion despite now knowing otherwise. "I want what I deserve."

"I've already disproved that, *Hector*," Sarah replied, still using a relatively pleasant voice despite the unpleasantness of the situation. "You do need help, but not from us."

"You dare mock me woman?" César asked, moving close enough to stare into the Andrews' matriarch's blue eyes.

"I'm not mocking you. I pity you," she replied. With that the older woman turned her back to him and crossed her arms, as if trying to give herself a hug. It was then that Sarah saw Ariel making the hand gesture some kids used to use when playing shooting games to indicate a weapon before holding up two fingers, silently attempting to warn her that both Fernandez and Evans were armed.

Sarah nodded in acknowledgment of the information. The couple behind her thankfully never saw the warning.

Now fuming mad, César grabbed Sarah Andrews by an arm with the hand that had not been holding his briefcase during the entire conversation, but whatever he was about to do next was stopped by an alarm going off.

"Dad!" shouted Ariel.

"Reginald!" screamed Sarah, breaking away from César to turn and look at her husband.

Everyone in the room looked toward the hospital bed.

Reginald Andrews' back briefly rose off the mattress as if pushed up from beneath, in unison with a foreboding spike on some of the monitor display's graph lines.

When they entered, Carol and César thought the man asleep. Had he been alert enough to know what was going on, hence this sudden reaction to his wife being roughly manhandled?

Various numbers and graphs were showing seriously dangerous readings. Some had even changed color to more redder hues as the collective equipment's respective noises now combined to make a continuous emergency signal.

Mother and daughter rushed to the man's side. Sarah on his right with Ariel on the opposite side of the bed as everything reached a critical crescendo.

"We're here dear," Sarah said, trying to hold back the tears. Her face was as close to the oxygen tent as it could be without breaking the seal and disturbing the air supply.

Then everything abruptly stopped.

The silence grew ominous as Reginald collapsed back onto the mattress faster than he rose.

The displays dropped with his body until everything both electronic and organic was totally still.

There was now only one continuous flat line traveling in the eerie muteness from left to right, accompanied above by a bunch of zeroes.

"Do something!" César ordered, moving closer to the bed.

The whole event had only taken a few fleeting seconds to happen but seemed a lot longer.

Regardless of actual duration, it would be one of the most traumatic in the Andrews family history.

Sarah took a step back and began to cry as Ariel reached under the oxygen tent and held her father's frail left hand in both of hers.

The physical remains of the man the world knew as Reginald Fredrick Andrews lay lifeless. The machines reflected this with their lack of activity.

"Not that. Revive him! Call an ambulance! His doctor!" Fernandez demanded, finally finding his voice again as Evans just stood back and contemplated her own future.

"No," Sarah solemnly said as she straightened upright with her back to him. "While you hastened his departure with your rough manners and outrageous demands, Reginald didn't wish the end of his existence prolonged either."

César wasn't sure what to do as he watched Ariel gently put her father's hand down. Then she pulled hers out of the tent and assumed a standing vigil position on her side of the hospital bed.

"Oh… Kay," Fernandez said, dragging the word out to two syllables as he stopped to think things over. "With him gone, maybe this makes things less complicated. As Reginald Andrews' heirs, you two and Fredrick can sign everything over to me even easier than when he was involved."

Sarah slowly turned around to face him and said, "You know what? This end's now."

Then the Andrews matriarch punched him in the nose as hard and as fast as she could.

CHAPTER 28

César Fernandez was caught totally off guard as fist met flesh. He never expected such a violent response, let alone an old woman like Sarah Andrews being able to move so fast or hit so hard.

The knuckles of her right hand crushed against his nostrils. The force of the blow damaged the now bleeding nasal cavity.

César raised his right arm. Whether in reflex toward the injury, as an attempt to punch his surprise opponent in return or to go for his weapon in its shoulder holster was unknown and didn't matter as Sarah grabbed his right wrist and shoved the connected hand against the man's lower jaw. While that only caused César to briefly bite his tongue and added further pain to his injury because of the abrupt movement, it also served as a good distraction as she grabbed Fernandez's gun before he could.

"Drop the briefcase and raise your hands," the elderly woman ordered, pointing the firearm at him.

"Si. Andale," he replied while complying.

+++

Carol Evans saw most of the action standing behind César.

At first, she was stunned. Everything had happened so quickly.

Discovering Reginald Andrews' current condition, let alone his sudden passing after going into cardiac arrest, were both great shocks. While surprised at the extreme reaction, part of her understood and could sympathize with the grieving new widow emotionally and physically lashing out, but not to this extent.

Yet it also finally dawned on Carol that she should be doing something to help and remembered there was a gun in her purse.

+++

While Fernandez's cryptic response puzzled her, the disguised Solitaire hadn't forgotten about the lady, nor Ariel's warning.

As Evans anxiously tried to open her purse, Solitaire could see by the way she fumbled with the catch that the personal assistant was neither a trained professional nor someone with a whole lot of firearm experience, but the Secret Samaritan had no plans to show any enemy mercy.

"Drop your purse to the ground and raise your hands or I'll use him for target practice," Solitaire said in a much deeper and younger female voice than that of Sarah Andrews.

Not knowing what else she could do, Evans obeyed the order, which angered César. "You should have pulled the trigger and worried about the consequences later," he snarled at her.

"She did the right thing. Now come towards us, slowly," said Solitaire.

Carol walked forward until she was standing next to César.

"Ariel, come here please," Solitaire requested in a much nicer tone.

When the Andrews Aviation executive was standing near, Solitaire handed her the gun. "Please keep this pointed at them," was the instruction before the Discrete Defender secured each prisoner's wrists behind their back with industrial strength zip ties pulled from her camouflage suit's utility belt— hidden under the dress borrowed from Sarah Andrews—to secure her prisoner.

Moments later Evans and Fernandez, now bound at the ankles too, were lying on the carpet.

Ariel watched the woman who still looked like her mother walk over to the hospital bed and asked "Where's Dad?"

"Your folks and Fredrick are safe in another room, along with your father's personal physician to monitor his condition and a couple of security guards," Solitaire answered. *At least being on chemo explains Reginald's missing mustache and weight loss.* "Sarah is on the other end of this," she added, pointing to the false hearing aid, "and kept me informed of things like Beatriz and Hector. In bed is just a Rescue Anne. A very modified CPR Dummy dressed up as your father. I controlled it and the monitors with a remote I have tucked up a dress sleeve," concluded the explanation, while she removed two long strips of cloth from underneath a blanket.

"And everyone else?" Ariel inquired, as the lady came back.

"Abbott was ordered to join the others the moment he finished showing you inside while the rest of the household staff were given the day off. The organization hates involving civilians but with Evans having been here before, we couldn't risk any substitutions in case she became suspicious, so thanks again for your cooperation," Solitaire explained, continuing the fiction that her current client was under about her being part of a team rather than a lone operative.

"Don't you dare," warned César, as she started to gag him. "My people—"

"It was only the three of us and a driver," Ariel said, as Solitaire finished her task. The cloth went across his mouth and its ends were knotted in back behind his head.

"I'll deal with him soon enough," the fake Sarah replied, as she gagged Carol too.

Then Ariel asked the question that had been on her mind since realizing she wasn't dealing with her real mother. "Iris Higgins, I presume?"

Evans' eyes widened in shock upon hearing that, but Solitaire couldn't answer as the sound of gunfire pierced the air.

+++

The chauffeured vehicle was still parked in front of the Andrews residence. To any observer, it looked as if the driver just casually sat behind the steering wheel with seat belt unfastened and waited patiently for his passengers to return.

In truth, Damián Garcia carefully watched his surroundings while listening to everything through the earpiece of the communications device César gave him earlier.

At first things were quiet. There was no sign of any guards or other people around. The conversation started out dull, but Garcia became more interested when his Jefe claimed to be the hombre's son.

When his announcement and demands were both rejected, Garcia grew concerned and knew it was time to act when Fernandez said "Andale," their code word to come rescue him.

The loyal Anbessa member reached over and undid the hidden catch below the seat cushion Carol Evans had occupied earlier. Inside the concealed compartment were nestled the components to a highly effective automatic rifle.

Bent down toward the front passenger foot well to work unobserved, Garcia had the weapon assembled and loaded in seconds. He then lowered the passenger window before removing the listening device to prevent it from becoming a possible distraction, so never heard his Jefe and the señorita

...Garcia stepped out of the car...

being bound and gagged.

Empty handed, Garcia then stepped out of the car as if to stretch his legs.

A brief walk around the vehicle's front allowed him to reach inside for the firearm left on the now closed seat cushion.

When the muzzle completely cleared the passenger window frame, Damián Garcia started running toward the house, firing at the entrance with every step.

+++

A gagged Fernandez looked like he was smiling as Ariel said, "Abbot always locks the front door after letting us in, and it has a solid steel inner liner for extra security."

"Yet even the best deadbolt will give eventually," realized Solitaire. Heading toward the study's lone entrance, she paused only long enough to retrieve Evans gun from where the open handbag fell.

However, the moment she picked up the weapon, something felt off.

Solitaire activated the magazine release, took one brief glance at the clip that was within and announced, "This weapon isn't loaded."

Her gag was the only thing that kept Carol from screaming while looking angrily at César.

"Keep them covered and silent. I'll take care of the driver," Solitaire advised, letting the empty gun fall back down to the floor as she left the study.

+++

Garcia cursed loudly that, despite concentrating his fire at the doorknob, he hadn't gotten through yet.

There was a hint of metal visible within some of the bullet holes, proving that his target was more than it appeared to be.

He tried slamming his body against the obstacle.

Although it still prevented entry, the fact that the door gave a little made Damián smile as he resumed firing.

+++

The foyer was empty.

All was silent within the house except for the sound of Solitaire's high heels rapidly clicking on the marble tile floor in a rush to her objective when something slammed against the front door.

She could see daylight beams through a few shots that had penetrated the outer edging beyond the steel liner, but how much longer the barrier would hold as the shooting resumed was unknown.

Solitaire paused a few feet away from the door, mentally assessing options. Her original plan was to stop the intruder the moment he broke into the house if the police—who Andrews' security staff were supposed to call the moment Ariel and her party entered the grounds—had not arrived by then.

That task was more difficult unarmed but could still be achieved by a well trained professional like herself.

+++

With weapon to one side, Damián Garcia slammed his body against the door again. His left shoulder grew sore, but the ache was worth it as the now vulnerable barrier finally gave way.

He entered the foyer and quickly rotated the rifle in every possible direction of attack.

Garcia held his fire until necessary to prevent accidentally hitting Fernandez or Evans, but the only one present was an old lady who approached him with a noticeable limp in her walk.

Although he aimed his weapon at her, she just kept shuffling toward him with small steps in that slow manner some elderly people displayed late in life. The woman reminded Garcia of his abuela. Gray hair, wrinkled and of stooped posture but still able to walk on her own unaided to an extent, although his grandmother wore her hearing aid in the right ear.

"Couldn't you have just rang the doorbell like a normal person?" the woman asked with a thick Southern accent and an attitude that matched his relative's as she came closer, either totally ignoring or unable to see the weapon he held. Whoever this woman was, her voice didn't match any of those heard during his eavesdropping.

"Where are they?" Garcia wanted to know, still looking around in case this might be a trap. He saw the staircase, the closed door near its base and the hallway leading into the rest of the residence, but they were the only two people in sight.

"Where are who?" the old woman asked in return.

"My Jefe and—"

"Don't know anyone named Jeffery."

Despite being armed, unfortunately rifles were best at longer ranges than near a potential target in the same room.

"Look lady," Garcia began, lowering the gun a little toward the floor so he could physically threaten her with his free hand.

Solitaire took that moment to grab the barrel with her left hand behind the muzzle while the right fist socked him hard in the throat.

Caught off guard, Damián desperately gasped for air, but managed to maintain possession of the rifle.

Garcia never knew that Solitaire risked letting go of the weapon to deliver a knife hand strike on either side of his neck with both hands simultaneously.

They struck the carotid arteries and interrupted the flow of oxygenated blood to his head.

Her opponent was still semi-conscious but now dizzy as he started falling toward the marble flooring.

Damián released the gun in hope of preventing a total descent by placing his hands ahead of him, palms down.

However, the bottom of his jaw met Solitaire's raised right knee as he fell, rendering the man completely helpless as he laid on the floor.

I'm not a big fan of repeating myself, but whatever works in an emergency, thought Solitaire as she pulled out two more zip ties and secured her prisoner.

Since Andrews Security officers were told not to engage the suspects until the police arrived, the sound of sirens growing louder through the open door meant Solitaire was now at risk of being asked questions that had to remain unanswered.

While her departure route was through the back of the house, she briefly returned to the study and told Ariel, "All the prisoners will be taken away momentarily. Be sure to tell the police everything with as much detail as you can, but please leave me and our agency out of it as much as possible. Where's that monitoring disc I gave you before we parted company at your office?"

Ariel replied, "I managed to hide it in the back of the car that brought me here."

"Good," said Solitaire. *No chance for recovery right now but thankfully if the authorities find it, they can't trace it back to me.* "Although I was nearby the whole time, you never activated its emergency call button for help. I'll go back to where you were held overnight and use that as a starting point to search for and recover your missing drone."

"Even if you have to destroy the prototype to keep it out of the wrong hands, please try to recover all our schematics and intellectual property on the XDS-1," requested Andrews. "I discovered before being kidnapped that Evans stole all our hard copy documentation and erased most of the computer files, which will put us back at least months if we have to attempt making another from scratch."

The Mysterious Samaritan was unable to respond as an authoritative voice shouted, "Freeze! Don't anyone move!"

Two armed police officers entered the study while a third remained in the open doorway with an estate security guard.

"The secured people are your prisoners, officer," Solitaire began, imitating Sarah Andrews voice again. "We're pressing charges against them for two different kidnappings and the theft of Andrews Aviation property."

"And who gift wrapped them for us?" one officer wondered, raising Evans while his partner helped Fernandez up off the floor so their legs could be cut free for easier transportation. While not department issue, the arms would remain zip tied until after they reached the police station.

"We're going to remove the gags so you can respond to your Miranda Rights and answer our questions," the officer told Fernandez as his partner addressed Evans.

"If you folks can excuse me for a moment, my daughter can begin the explanations while I go check on my sick husband," replied Sarah.

"He's dying," the estate guard whispered to the man next to him.

"Err, okay. But please be as quick as possible," the officer by the door requested, as he moved to let the elderly lady out.

"I will," promised Sarah, as she started to leave the room.

"Stop her you idiots!" a now ungagged César protested. "She's—"

"Don't bother listening to that estúpido bufón," Carol said the moment her mouth was clear, interrupting her now ex-boyfriend as the two entered into a heated verbal argument.

Needing to break up the dispute, the authorities would never discover that Sarah Andrews returned for her interview after she had left the premises via the rear delivery gate driving a white van.

CHAPTER 29

When informed by their attorney that the arrested Fernandez and Garcia faced serious multiple charges, the rest of the Anbessas gathered and prepared for the worse at their main den on the outskirts of downtown Miami. Every soldier was well armed and their headquarters secured in case the police decided to raid them next after their leader's casa was searched.

The bail set for César was exorbitant, but could have been paid that evening if anyone knew what happened to the ransom collected earlier that week. Yet even if the gang had the money to get him released, the police were exercising their legal rights to hold Fernandez for questioning on several other open investigations, which delayed his freedom.

Despite the charges against him, Damián Garcia could have already been arraigned and released pending trial. Yet ever loyal, he refused to leave his

Jefe alone in jail.

Nobody knew or cared what happened to César's lady. She was an outsider and unimportant, compared to the fate of the Lions.

+++

Solitaire's attempt to search Fernandez's residence was a bust.

After pausing in route to change disguises so its driver appeared more nondescript, by the time Solitaire's white van pulled near, the place was surrounded by patrol cars and other official looking vehicles, indicating there might be more agencies interested in the Anbessas besides the Miami Police Department.

With a polite wave at the officer directing traffic, the brown-haired soccer mom drove past the potential crime scene. After patronizing the drive-thru window of a fast-food establishment, Solitaire sat in her van and initiated additional data searches on a computer tablet while eating.

The results led to parking a few blocks away from the Anbessas' den later that evening because while all of César's listed assets were legitimate, records showed his mother had purchased that building a month *after* her passing.

It was a rather nondescript structure. Just another warehouse among many in this area. There was no evidence that anyone had ever noticed its lack of signage or any indication of what business might be using the facility.

As the sun set upon the Gulf Coast, one shadow moved within the growing darkness. Dressed in her gray camouflage suit, Solitaire crouched behind the waist high parapet wall of the building closest to her target.

Gloved hands held what looked like one of the more advanced cellphones commercially available, but it was really the remote-control unit for her reconnaissance drone.

Silently hovering well over the enemy's heads to avoid being seen, its camera broadcast showed five men–each bearing an automatic rifle–on the other side of the alley. One at each corner of the warehouse's rectangular roof along with a man near the lone fire escape. With each dependent upon the ambient city light, none possessed a flashlight that would risk giving away their positions. There wasn't enough illumination present to read by or make out fine details, but one was able to see everything needed for guard duty.

The special lenses built into her camouflage suit's hood were light sensitive and automatically adjusted to viewing conditions, which allowed Solitaire to see in the dark.

Diagonally behind and to the right of the warehouse's air conditioning unit, the building's upmost access door sat relatively dead center of the rectangle, with the fire escape to its right. While its door faced Solitaire and the alley, thankfully every sentry except the one closest in the lower left-hand corner currently had their backs to her position.

After double checking the equipment within the compartments and externally attached to her suit's utility belt, along with the extra from the van lying on the tar and gravel surface around her, Solitaire sent the drone into action.

+++

Juan stood watch like the rest of the gang but was thankful to have a quiet corner over the alley. With his Novia pregnant, he had been seriously thinking about quitting the Anbessas—if they'd let him—and finding a more legitimate job. Provided there was one that paid at least as good as the Lions and he survived the siege everyone was afraid of and prepared for.

The man became momentarily alarmed when something flew in front of him, but relaxed upon realizing what it was.

"Alberto, you loco…" Juan began in a low voice to prevent getting an amigo in trouble. "Jefe said to keep that drone locked up in his safe."

Alberto and the safe, thought Solitaire, reading his lips on the monitor image as she pressed a touch screen button.

Juan realized his mistake too late as a projectile shot out from the drone and hit him in the neck. Before he could say anything, his unconscious body fell onto the roof.

Solitaire raised the device again and studied the other four but if any of them were aware of what happened, they gave no indication as each continued maintaining their position.

The drone only has one sleeping gas dart left so I better save it, she thought, while recalling the unit to her roof.

After it landed safely, Solitaire put the recon drone on standby mode to conserve power and secured the remote control in its padded pouch on her utility belt.

With that she grabbed the coil of strong, black hued rope at her feet. A four-prong ebony grappling hook was tied to one end. The other was connected to a ratchet-like device attached to the base of a protruding roof exhaust pipe beside her.

There were a couple of different launch mechanisms that could have been used, but the Mysterious Samaritan decided on the simplest that required no additional equipment. She stood and twirled the hook in the air for a couple of spins like a lasso before throwing it.

Its steel claws sailed across the man-made chasm before landing on target next to the sleeping gang member's feet. She paused and waited to make sure her work went unnoticed.

Upon confirming that, Solitaire reached down and started turning the ratchet's noiseless crank to reel in the excess rope until a hook barb was caught on the other building's parapet.

Although the grappler was specially padded to reduce any possible noise, Solitaire waited a moment to make sure the other guards still remained unaware of her actions.

After double checking that the line was taut and the load within and on her utility belt was symmetrical, she started walking across the alley on her makeshift tight rope.

Although a pole would have increased rotational inertia to help balance her central mass, with empty arms outstretched Solitaire took each step carefully in a measured but steady pace to reach the other side quickly and safely before there was any risk of being spotted.

Solitaire's shoes were durable for potential, combat but flexible enough to feel the rope beneath her covered soles. Despite having a stabilizing steel core, the rope's nylon exterior could still twist against the walker as it stretched and relaxed in contrast to where her feet were at any given moment. Having a gymnast's slim body also helped.

She was careful to brace and lean into the wind whenever necessary. The breeze was strong but steady, gusty at times since the weather forecast predicted possible showers overnight with the remnants of the last tropical system still offshore. Yet the skies were relatively clear, for now.

Her departure point and destination were both only three stories high, but a fall would still be serious even without Anbessas sentries posted at the rear exterior corners of their headquarters to watch the alley.

A little over halfway across Solitaire had to stop in mid-step as the roof sentry in the other corner watching the alley suddenly moved.

She slowly lowered the leg to secure her footing on the rope without having any movement attract attention. Concern grew and options raced through her mind in case the man turned around and noticed there was now one guard less on duty.

His head turned from side to side, checking out something below.

Moments later the sentry grew still, his gaze still on the alley.

Figuring it must have been nothing because if he had truly spotted something there would have been further action, Solitaire was about to continue when a crosswind caught her off guard!

She fought a brief but lost cause to maintain her balance before slipping off the rope.

Gravity was quick to attempt claiming a new victim. However, Solitaire remained silent and concentrated on catching the line in her gloved hands.

The left managed to grab it first. Fingers tightened their life saving grip as she moved her right hand to follow suit.

When both firmly held the rope, Solitaire raised her legs. The right hooked itself around the nylon cord before the left, yet all four limbs now grasped the tightrope.

Her back faced the alley below, her feet the departure point. By alternating one hand in front of the other, Solitaire pulled herself along until the top of her head touched the other building.

For a moment she was only secured by just the lower body as Solitaire let go of the rope and pulled herself up and over the parapet onto the enemy's roof.

Although he would still be out for at least a couple of more hours, the hands of the unconscious man were quickly zip tied together behind his back. The rifle was replaced where it lay after being unloaded. Its magazine quietly left nearby, but not in immediate view should it be searched for.

From her position she saw there were still the two guards in the upper corners, although the left's view of everything behind him was blocked by the building's air conditioner and roof access. Everyone on the right could see each other when needed but were paying more attention to their individual posts at the moment.

Hoping to avoid further enemy contact, Solitaire moved toward the AC Unit, careful not to slip on or kick any loose roof gravel, for that would risk giving her presence away.

Near its intake vent, she took a multi-tool from her utility belt and selected the proper screwdriver option to undo the grill cover.

With three screws completely removed, Solitaire loosened the bottom left one just enough to rotate the cover down until it touched the roof. She then removed the canister externally attached to her belt at each hip.

Solitaire placed them within the vent opening, their nozzles pointed inward. Once activated, an aerosol propelled mist sprayed out of each container and started turning green as it mixed with the surrounding oxygen. There was no backwash as the system started drawing her sleeping gas into the building.

Provided no one has a window open, it will take a few minutes to circulate through the third floor, she thought while replacing the grill cover. *Longer for the rest of the building, but I'll be safe thanks to the special air filtration system built into my mask.*

With that task accomplished, Solitaire stood and started working her way toward the access door to enter the building. *Fernandez's private safe has to be in his office somewhere on three. Despite finding nothing but the architect's original blueprints for this place online, I can't picture it being on a lower floor. Once I have the XDS-1 and its records, an anonymous tip to the police will allow them to serve any possible warrants they might have on the Anbessas here for the lions sleep tonight.*

Yet that was not a completely accurate statement.

There were still the four remaining guards on the roof to avoid, and whoever was coming out of the roof access!

CHAPTER 30

Solitaire froze. Her camouflage suit blending with the dark shadows kept her from being immediately noticed, for she was not completely hidden behind the door. Thankfully the man didn't open it fully, for there was no way to prevent physical contact discovery.

He was only a few inches taller than her and, except for it being slung over his left shoulder instead of held, armed like the other Anbessas.

Without hesitation Solitaire retrieved a short, leather covered club-like object from where it hung dead center on the utility belt near the small of her back.

A quick glance to her left confirmed the guard at the fire escape wasn't looking in their direction. Then Solitaire swung the weapon at the back of the new arrival's head.

The heavy end of the blackjack struck and rendered the man helpless, but as she moved to grab the slumping body, his rifle slipped off the left shoulder and discharged as it hit the roof!

The shot struck to the right of the man at the fire escape, barely missing his feet.

With the sentry yelling that he was under attack, Solitaire gave up any hope of remaining undiscovered as she dropped the unconscious man and ran into the open roof access, closing the door behind her.

Cursing the fact that the rifle's safety must have been off, Solitaire used the metal bar that was resting against one wall of the interior landing to secure the door as the sound of running feet grew louder. She then quickly descended the short staircase.

The top of her head was just a step below being level with the roof as the banging of fists upon the metal door was replaced with a hail of bullets from at least two automatic rifles.

The barrier looked like Swiss cheese after the last shot. Its metal bar was split in two with just an end hanging in each latch, but the door still stood as the enemy used brute force to finish smashing it open.

Solitaire waited three steps down from her previous position with a handful of small green pellets taken from her utility belt.

As the door broke away from its frame, she threw the minuscule objects at the enemy.

The force of impact caused green sleeping gas to burst forth from each projectile as their soft shells broke against something hard. Coughs and curses were heard as the metal object slid down the stairs.

The Clandestine Crusader timed a short vertical jump so she landed on the busted barrier just when it would have crashed into her. Solitaire turned to face the third floor below as she rode on the door like a makeshift surfboard.

At the bottom step she jumped off into the open hallway. Her board didn't stop until it slid across the floor and crashed, embedding itself deep into the sheet rock of the opposing wall.

A look around to get her bearings revealed a hint of green filled the air, an indication that the sleeping gas was doing well despite not seeing anyone snoozing.

Solitaire saw another staircase at the opposite end of the hall. Every door along each side of the corridor was closed, but none bore any markings of what awaited behind them.

The one next to where her surfboard wiped out was unlocked and turned out to be a janitor's closet. The broken door had knocked over a shelving unit full of cleaning supplies, but that wasn't her concern.

The first room on the right was also unsecured and looked like someone's personal quarters. There was an empty full-size bed and an overstuffed tote bag sitting on the floor at the base of the room's lone window, but no occupants. A quick search of the bag revealed nothing but assorted men's clothing without any proof of ownership. Otherwise, the room was completely bare with no hint of a safe.

The next door on the left, several feet away from the janitor's, was locked.

With the skill of a professional locksmith, a few thin picks from her utility belt moved the doorknob's inner tumblers to their proper positions without the actual key. Seconds later Solitaire was within what had to be César Fernandez's private office, for a framed oversize photograph of the man wearing an elegant business suit hung on the opposite wall, facing anyone who entered.

I've seen larger, thought Solitaire, looking around the small space. Yet while lacking in size, the office décor was as extravagant as any upper executives.

So that Fernandez could see everyone within, a well polished mahogany desk sat at an odd angle in the far-left hand corner on the thick plush rug that lined the rectangular shaped room. A couch covered the length of the opposite wall on the right. Except for a map of Miami that could be seen while seated at the desk and the self portrait, the rest of the art on the walls featured a variety of naked women in lewd poses.

Yet what interested Solitaire most was the free standing safe.

Next to the leather-bound executive desk chair, it stood about four feet high by almost two feet wide, aligned with the wall corners behind the desk. Its exterior looked at least an inch thick. A three-handle flywheel sat dead center on a door with interior hinges. Above that was a classic combination lock whose dial numbers went from zero through ninety-nine, with a red line on the center of its outer ring to indicate digital position.

Hmm... A safe this size will have at least six digits in the combination but while set to whatever the customer wanted upon delivery, it's only a fifty-fifty chance of clockwise or counterclockwise for each number, realized Solitaire as she removed items from utility belt pouches on each hip.

Soon a device no larger than an unopened deck of playing cards rested in her left gloved hand. From its top ran a cord to a suction cup positioned as close to the lock as possible. The sensor within the cup monitored every minute dial movement as Solitaire's right hand rotated the knob through its range. When the correct number was reached, a small red light turned green. A liquid crystal display recorded each digit of the combination until the memory was cleared.

The sequence not only went against tradition and started counterclockwise, it also alternated directions in an irregular pattern. Only the ninth and final number turned out to be a single digit as the green light started blinking to indicate the safe had been successfully opened.

Solitaire turned the flywheel and pulled on its handles.

As the door swung left toward the wall, inside was a small shelf near the top, with the rest of the safe open storage space.

Yet the XDS-1 prototype wasn't there!

CHAPTER 31

I guess there really is no honor among thieves. Did that Alberto or someone else decide to go into business for themselves? Solitaire wondered as she searched the safe for clues.

On the shelf was a couple of bundled money stacks, each composed of only American $100 bills. *There's got to be at least a good $30,000 here,* Solitaire figured, before putting the money back in the safe after making sure there was nothing behind it.

There were also two passports, both issued by the United States. One was in César Fernández's name while the other bore an alias, but each had a picture of the arrested gang leader. *Prepared for a possible quick escape,* she surmised. A miniature digital camera among her possessions took a quick photograph of each. Then she replaced them and continued searching.

Along the bottom were detailed schematics for several automatic weapons, indicating possible ghost gun manufacturing on the lower floors.

Yet other than one empty file folder that bore the Andrews Aviation corporate logo, there was no proof that the Lions ever had the stolen drone, let alone where it was now.

Concluding her search, Solitaire closed and locked the safe. When the police were anonymously summoned later, the call would also include the combination.

Odd. No computer, she thought, taking another look at Fernandez's empty desk. *Not even a potential paper trail. It's not as if gangs keep employment and tax records, but they must keep track of the important data somehow. Time to search the lower floors.*

Locking the office on her way out, Solitaire crept toward the end of the hallway. She was about to try the door on the right in front of the stairwell but stopped in mid step.

Much to her surprise, there were voices coming from the floor below!

With her back against the wall next to the staircase, Solitaire took a quick but discrete look down the stairwell and saw through the sleeping gas the distinctive shape of two men with active flashlights.

"I don't like this man," one male voice said in Spanish, using his light to attempt seeing through the artificial mist.

"Si," agreed the other as Solitaire pulled back, understanding every word. "This weird green stuff knocks everyone out, but it ain't tear gas and there's no sign of the cops. Yet so far, no rival's soldiers have attempted to take us either."

"Yeah. Odd," agreed the first. "I just wish Jefe had bought more gas masks, but he says their purchase is monitored nowadays."

"At least the two of us and everyone outside are still awake," pointed out the other man.

Except for your amigos on the roof, thought Solitaire, thankful that the gas masks necessitated the need to use a louder than normal speaking volume. The men's voices, while a bit muffled, were still understandable.

"Okay. I'll take this floor, and you search three," the second man said, before Solitaire heard footsteps on the staircase.

No time to check out the last room, for whoever is coming up will have a clear view of it at any moment. Only one option left, realized Solitaire.

+++

As he cradled his rifle against his chest, Bernardo Perez wouldn't publicly admit to being scared. He only joined the Anbessas after graduating high school last month as a way to earn quick money instead of getting a menial job like his parents or going into massive debt for a college degree. Until tonight, his hopes of having an easy life had come true. His only responsibilities with the Lions were just guard duty and fetching food orders when the others were hungry.

Yet now things were getting far more serious than Perez ever expected. The last thing he wanted was to be hurt or killed, let alone become a potential target because of the weapon in his hand.

Maybe doing construction work with my padre won't be so bad after all, but I've got to get out of here alive first, he realized, while taking the staircase one cautious step at a time.

When eye level with the third floor, Perez shined his flashlight around the area ahead and noted nothing in sight.

All was quiet. *Like a graveyard,* was his gloomy thought.

After another step, Perez moved his body to the far left of the staircase, like he saw officers do on some police shows. This put the end corner of the hallway straight ahead and gave him an angled view of the corridor. The fact it remained empty made Bernardo happy as he continued upward.

When the weapon cleared the top step, Perez leaned forward and saw nothing amiss down the hallway except the green gas that filled the air.

Once completely on the third floor he opened the door in front of him, but there was only a table surrounded by a bunch of chairs in an otherwise empty room.

Perez knew the first door on his right was César Fernandez's office. With a quick check to make sure it was locked, he moved on.

Through the tinted air, any evidence of Solitaire's arrival remained unnoticed as Perez opened the door on his left before the roof access staircase.

Inside what many called the Bunk Room was a lone figure asleep on the full-size bed.

"Hey amigo!" Perez called out in Spanish as he approached. "Can you wake up?"

The only response was someone attacking him from behind.

Solid blows struck both his right shoulder and arm near the wrist at the same time.

In reflex, Bernardo took a step to his left in hope of striking back, but lost possession of his rifle in the process.

Yet had he managed to pull the trigger, Perez wasn't sure a shot would have done any good against whatever was in front of him.

Besides being barely able to make out that someone or some thing was standing in front of him even with the flashlight shining directly at the shadowy figure, his assailant had no visible facial features, which made him ask in English, "What kind of a man are you?"

"Don't move," a weird voice replied in Spanish, as the faceless one pointed the weapon at him. "Drop the flashlight and raise your hands," it added in English.

"Si," Perez said, complying with the request. The light flickered as it hit the floor but stayed on as it rolled off to one side. Yet Bernardo couldn't help wondering *I don't see a gas mask. How can this guy be breathing and not fall asleep? Let alone, why is this hombre using one of those trick voice changers to keep anyone from recognizing his voice?*

"Answer all my questions and you will live to see another day," the figure promised.

"Si. What do you want to know?"

"Where's Alberto?"

That was a surprise. "The Eagle?" Perez asked in return. "When Damián Garcia sounded the alarm that we needed to gather here and protect what's ours, Alberto said that his Madre was ill but promised to be here as soon as he could. But he hasn't shown up yet." *Unless I'm really talking to him right now, but why the games?*

"Is Alberto's last name Aguilar?" Solitaire's altered voice asked, since Aguila was Spanish for eagle.

"Si," Perez answered.

"Where does he live?" Solitaire wanted to know.

"Honestly, I don't know," swore Perez. "Only the higher Jefes have that stuff."

"Hold still," ordered the shadowy figure.

"Por favor. Please don't kill me," begged Perez, staring at the gun still pointed at him.

Solitaire's reply was to reach out with her free hand and remove the gas mask from the man in front of her.

Bernardo Perez tried to hold his breath, but still passed out and slumped to the floor in less than a minute.

+++

Whew! Solitaire silently exclaimed as she lowered the rifle. *It's a good thing that guy didn't try calling my bluff. When his flashlight blinded me, the camouflage suit's built in night vision lenses needed time to readjust themselves. Not only couldn't I guarantee any shot's accuracy, but I prefer to only shoot in self defense.*

Fully able to see again, she unloaded the weapon and put everything on the bed next to the duffle bag draped with a shirt and pants to look like someone asleep in the green mist.

Fernandez probably called his lawyer, but Garcia must have used his one phone call to warn the rest of the gang, surmised Solitaire. *In any event, it's time to get out of here and go eagle hunting.*

First, I better make sure the coast is clear, she thought, standing next to the roof access staircase. Soon its remote control was within gloved hands as she summoned her reconnaissance drone.

On the neighboring building's rooftop, the device reactivated and took to the sky. However, the transmitted surveillance camera images received moments later were not good.

The man near my tight rope is still unconscious, but only two out of the remaining four are asleep too. One's watching the roof exit, and the other is nowhere in sight. Probably went down the fire escape to get help, which means it's time for me to get the hell out of here!

CHAPTER 32

Solitaire quietly raced up the stairs, yet stopped when she was eye level with the roof's rough surface.

One lone guard was standing a few feet away in front of the exit, his rifle aimed directly at the doorless access.

Solitaire saw the grim look on the man's face and wondered, *Do they want prisoners for questioning, or will trespassers be shot on sight?*

She could see everything clearly through her suit hood's night vision lenses. Being one of the original roof sentries, he was still dependent on just the surrounding ambient city light, but there was no way the man could miss seeing anyone emerge from the building.

Except, with the suit's unique camouflage color scheme blending with the darkness, maybe her if she was extremely careful and quiet. *Yet why take the chance when I don't have to?* Solitaire asked herself while pushing a few icons on the remote-control screen.

She stood on the next step and watched the man stare intently in her direction. Solitaire knew he couldn't see her, but it still felt odd having him there.

Suddenly the man moved.

He stood fully erect, then fell forward as the recon drone's remaining tranquilizer dart took effect and knocked him unconscious.

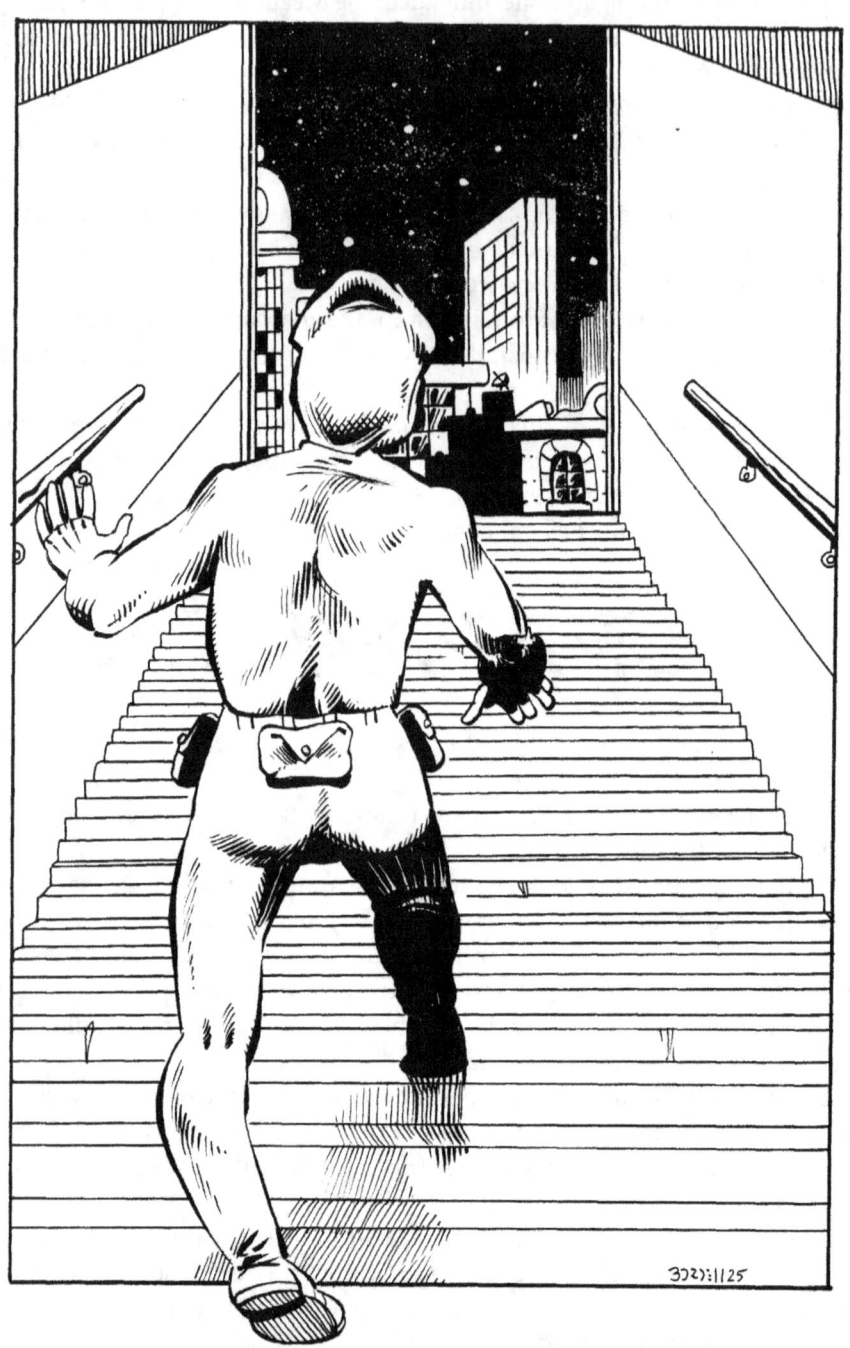

Solitaire quickly but quietly raced up the stairs...

With that Solitaire pushed one last icon before putting the remote control back in its designated utility belt pouch.

Then she raced up the remaining steps and out onto the roof. Her feet touched tarred gravel, accompanied by the sounds of people rapidly climbing up the fire escape as the drone carried out its last instruction.

Whoever had reached the top of the fire escape first shouted in Spanish "I see him!" as Solitaire ran for the corner where she arrived.

She knew there was no time to attempt another tight rope walk even before a shot hit the roof, barely missing her feet.

Instead, Solitaire grabbed the barbed hook from where it had supported her trip across the alley and grasped it firmly in both hands as she jumped off the building's parapet.

She leapt at an angle away from both departure point and the other warehouse where the rope was anchored.

"That hombre's loco!" the Secret Samaritan heard someone yell in Spanish as she started to fall.

Gravity tugged at Solitaire's limp form, but it would not win this battle as the rope grew taut.

As she hit the bottom of her swing, the length needed to span the alley put her level with the second floor of the warehouses surrounding that intersection.

Solitaire repositioned her body to maximize momentum, which created more lift as she swung toward the top of her brief flight arch.

When she cleared the windows facing the back street both buildings shared, the apex of Solitaire's swing put her just above the upper edge of the other warehouse.

The Clandestine Crusader let go of the rope and spun to her left, barely clearing the top of that structure's facade.

Solitaire landed on her left side but continued rolling for a couple of more feet across the tarred gravel surface until her momentum was spent.

Not one of my more gracious landings, but—

The thought was interrupted by a gun shot that landed just inches from her concealed face.

Solitaire instantly scrambled for cover as a second shot struck closer to where she was.

Behind the parapet from which the tight rope walk started, Solitaire withdrew a handful of gray pellets from a pouch on her utility belt.

They broke upon being flung at the rough surface she laid on.

Instead of more sleeping gas, the released chemicals mixed with the surrounding oxygen and created a thick smoke screen.

Even though there's no breeze, unfortunately it won't last long in such an open area, realized Solitaire as she turned around on her hands and knees. After crawling a couple of feet away from the newly created diversion, she rose and started sprinting toward the other side of the building as fast as she could.

+++

Once off the fire escape, one of the Anbessas hastily checked on their unconscious members as another took the lookout position at the corner where the intruder disappeared. Between being stuck using an older rifle he didn't like and his inability to get a decent shot at a moving target, the man could only stand there and watched in amazement as the enemy miraculously made it across the alley and disappeared from sight on the opposing roof.

The rest of those who had made the ascent were now hastily trying to get back down again, but couldn't go through the building because of whatever that green smoke was.

Concurrently, the Lion's street level sentries had started searching the surrounding area for whatever might be left of the intruder.

"Did you see where he went Pedro?" someone below loudly yelled in Spanish.

"Yes! There!" was Pedro's shouted reply, while pointing to the warehouse directly across from him. Two shots had missed before the black smoke appeared, making the gang member wonder about the rifle's sights because his aim couldn't have been off that badly.

"Seriously?" the man below yelled back as he stared up at the neighboring building.

No one at street level could see the black smoke rising from the rooftop and Pedro, not knowing what to think, lowered his weapon and remained silent about it.

+++

Solitaire never questioned why the firing stopped as she ran in a straight line that kept the smoke screen between her and the Anbessas, gaining speed with each step as the other end of the rooftop drew near.

At the far side she never broke stride. One small hop put her onto the parapet edge and a strong jump sent her flying into the air!

Solitaire caught one brief glimpse of gang members gathering at the base of the warehouse's fire escape down below as she stretched her body out to its full length. Then she hooked her arms behind her knees to form a makeshift ball and started tumbling forward through nothing but empty space.

Gravity pulled her form closer to the ground with each passing second, despite the fact that every somersault roll also put Solitaire further across the alley.

After tense moments of free fall flight, her back landed upon the roof of the two-story building next to the three tiered one she had jumped from.

As she completed her next roll Solitaire released her arms. Momentum carried her to an upright position from which she kept running.

It was not at her best speed, but Solitaire made it across the roof and started down that building's fire escape. *Don't feel anything sprained or broken, but I'll probably be sore in the morning. Still a bit shaky because I've never done anything like that before, but I've got to get out of here while I still can because it's just a matter of time until the Anbessas discover that roof is empty and decide to widen their search area.*

She kept to the shadows during her walk through the rear service alley, ever alert to anyone nearby, but there were no Lions on the prowl. *I traveled a good four blocks going cross building and the van's just up ahead.*

Behind a local delivery service was parked a fleet of white vans. The fact an extra vehicle was among them went unnoticed as Solitaire crept up to hers and opened the rear door with the key from her utility belt.

Once inside, she saw her recon drone had returned through the screenless air vent in the roof and was now sitting on its recharging base. After closing the hatch and securing the drone, she made a quick but anonymous phone call to the police using a different voice changer than the one in her camouflage suit. The computer voice was artificial but sounded as human as technically possible as someone claiming to be a member of the Anbessas gang wanted to surrender to the authorities, including giving them the combination to César Fernandez's office safe as proof of his sincerity.

Simultaneously, Solitaire was changing clothes. Her special operations suit and its utility belt were soon within separate storage containers until the uniform could be examined for damage and the accessory restocked as a rather plain looking woman made her way to the front of the van to occupy the driver's seat after sitting a computer tablet screen down on the passenger seat.

Like most men against an unidentified opponent, I was glad to hear the Lions automatically assumed they were fighting a man. Meaning they won't be looking for a lady, let alone me, happily thought Solitaire. *But now it's time to find a wayward eagle.*

CHAPTER 33

A fter moving to a public shopping center parking space a couple of miles away from the Anbessas' den, Solitaire started using her computer tablet.

Fingertips flew across icons representing board keys as the resulting information was displayed on the screen.

Even if he only has a cell and I eliminate the land lines, there are still too many Albertos and A. Aguilars in the directories to know which is him, she realized. *Time to try another tactic. If he is the Lion's tech guy, let's see if he has any technical journal subscriptions.*

Comparing various publication databases against local listings finally narrowed the possibilities down to just one. Solitaire double checked the address against driver's license records before she reviewed what was within the van to use while contemplating her next move.

+++

The address was within a suburban neighborhood a few miles from the shopping center. Solitaire left her van parked a couple of houses away and walked the short distance to her target, but stopped to look at a well maintained motorcycle with leather seating and dual chrome exhaust pipes parked at the curb in front of her destination.

There was no record of a sidecar, but that's Alberto's cycle, Solitaire discovered when she checked the license plate. *They don't really match but it's a nice bike,* she thought while briefly examining the engine after making sure there were no potential witnesses about. *Looks like he's packing to bug out, but no sign of the XDS-1 in there,* was the results of visually scanning the sidecar's interior. *Time to enact my original plan.*

The disguised Solitaire walked up to the front porch. Despite it being almost eleven that night, the light over the entrance was still on. She stood off to one side of the welcome mat that lay before the closed screen door in case she received an unfriendly reception and rang the bell.

"Uno momento, por favor," a female voice within the residence called out in Spanish.

The inner door opened just what the security chain allowed. Through the gap Solitaire saw a hint of a Hispanic lady in her late fifties, with black hair turning gray and wrinkles around alert brown eyes. "¿Cómo puedo ayudarte?" she said, asking if the visitor needed help.

"Si. ¿Alberto está en casa?" Solitaire said in Spanish as she watched the lady's eyes widen in surprise at being asked if Alberto was home. "My name is Rosa. We were supposed to have a date tonight, but he never showed."

The woman behind the door looked over the red-haired visitor. She was rather plain, but not in an ugly way despite wearing an unflattering dark blue dress that did nothing to accent her womanly curves. The drab black handbag over the left shoulder didn't match the outfit.

Yet the lady's smile grew as wide as her eyes as she quickly opened her house to let Rosa in while speaking in rapid fire Spanish. "I'm sorry. You just caught me by surprise. I thought that son of mine would never get his head out of his computers long enough to realize there was a real world around him. Let alone women. I'm Violeta Aguilar, his mother. Feel free to call me Vi. Mrs. Aguilar is so formal. Come in. Come in. How long have you two known each other?," she added happily as Rosa entered.

"Just a couple of weeks," lied Solitaire, looking around the modest living room and its meager furnishings. *If Alberto is making money being with the Anbessas, he's not sharing it with his family.*

"So, you work with him at that computer firm downtown?" wondered Violeta.

"Si," *if that's who you think he's employed by.* "Anyway, I just wanted to make sure he was all right."

"I'm sorry that he didn't keep his date with you, but Alberto came home, said he had an important project to work on and has been in his room ever since," explained his mother.

"Oh? Being in a different department, I didn't know. Most of our time together at work is either in the break room or in hallways chatting. Last time I saw him today was shortly after lunch," Solitaire replied, covering herself before Violeta got suspicious.

"Well, let me show you to his room so you two can talk," Mrs. Aguilar said happily.

"Gracias Vi," Solitaire said as she wondered if his mother was expecting Alberto and Rosa to get married and give her grandchildren.

Violeta led them from the living room across a short hall to a closed door.

"Hijo," Violeta called out to her son as she knocked on the wooden barrier.

"Madre, I told you I'm busy," shouted a deep male voice from the other side in Spanish.

Solitaire thought she heard the muffled background noise of someone hastily packing, but remained silent as Violeta said, "Si Alberto, but I thought you'd want to know Rosa is here."

"¿Qué?" asked Alberto.

"Rosa. Your girlfriend," his mother said happily, looking at the lady standing next to her.

Then Solitaire grew concerned as any noise coming from the other side of the door suddenly stopped.

Ignoring her hostess, she moved forward and tried the knob. The door was not locked, but opening it revealed a Hispanic male wearing a t-shirt, bluejeans and sneakers climbing out of a window with something in his hands, leaving an open suitcase half full on the bed.

"¡Alberto!" screamed Violeta, confused and shocked to see her son fleeing as Solitaire turned to run back to the front door.

Crossing the doorstep, Solitaire saw Alberto hastily toss two laptop bags and what looked like a square box into the sidecar before circling around the back of the motorcycle.

Not bothering to pause and put on the helmet that rested against the rear of the seat, Alberto mounted the bike and tried starting the engine as the unknown woman ran toward him.

It wouldn't start.

"Damn it!" Alberto cursed as he got off, keeping the uncooperative motorcycle between him and the stranger who approached the sidecar.

"¡Back off Chicha!" he snarled at her in Spanish with his right fist raised, ready to fight as the left hand went behind his back.

"All I want is the XDS-1 drone and its data the Anbessas' stole from Andrews Aviation," Solitaire replied in Spanish as she started to reach into the sidecar.

"¡Oh hell no!" shouted the black-haired man as he pulled out a switchblade knife from its rear holster on his left hip. Its three-inch-long blade sprung out at the push of a button and slashed the air in front of Solitaire's face.

She was forced to take a step back, then dodge to her left.

Any knife was a dangerous weapon, even in inexperienced hands. Just a two-inch blade was sufficient enough to penetrate the human body and strike a vital organ in one blow. The way he started to slash at her again— but quickly changed the knife's direction in mid stroke to further press the attack—showed Solitaire that Alberto knew how to properly use his weapon. She thought of various ways to defeat a southpaw opponent as her left shoulder slumped to let the handbag drop down to her waiting hand.

"That technology is my ticket out of here," Alberto said, keeping the knife in front of him as his right hand reached for the box on top of the stuff in the sidecar. "If I can't make more of these on my own, I'll sell it to the highest bidder and live in style the rest of my life."

"I don't think so," Solitaire replied, as she swung the purse around and hit his right hand hard with it.

"¡Damn!" Alberto screamed, surprised that such a relatively small handbag could hurt so much upon impact, not knowing about the small steel plate

Solitaire had within the lining of each long side.

Unable to immediately obtain his objective, Aguilar moved to slash at the woman again and force her away from the sidecar, but his target was ready as Solitaire avoided the knife by bringing her right hand up and under Alberto's left to grab his wrist.

There was no hesitation in her actions as Solitaire quickly moved his wrist back at an angle it was never meant to assume.

Alberto screamed in pain and was forced to let go of the knife as he felt something within at least tear, if not break outright.

Yet that didn't stop him from trying to punch the woman with his right fist.

Solitaire raised her purse like a shield. While none of his knuckles broke, Alberto knew he had hit something hard while her right fist slugged him.

Dazed, Aguilar took a step back in hope of buying a moment to attempt recovering, but Solitaire didn't hesitate and grabbed his right arm.

Before he could react, Alberto's right wrist was being zip tied to the motorcycle's left handlebar. Then Solitaire pulled another plastic restraint out of her purse and secured Aguilar's left wrist to the right handlebar.

"Now then, I'm taking the XDS-1," she repeated, removing the top item out of the sidecar.

The container was nothing more than a wooden box with an attached hinged lid from an unknown source that had been repurposed for the occasion. Inside, wrapped within a couple of t-shirts for padding, was the stolen drone.

Solitaire closed the box and placed it on the ground behind her. But as she reached back inside the sidecar to figure out which was the right computer that contained Ariel Andrews' missing information and research, Alberto said, "Wait. Maybe we can make a deal."

She stared at him and said, "I'm listening," while unsealing the first laptop bag.

"The computer in your hands has all the information our Jefe's inside man stole from Andrews Aviation that helped us get that thing," revealed Alberto, not knowing that the man was really César Fernandez's girlfriend. "The other is mine and it has all the Anbessas' personal data, from Ghost Gun blueprints to sales' clients and records. Let me go with all the Andrews' stuff and it's yours."

"Why would your boss want to keep all that incriminating evidence?" Solitaire wondered.

"He doesn't know I have it. It's my insurance policy. Being their tech guy, I keep track of all the Anbessas data. I've got information on spreadsheets dating back to the day I joined the gang. Think of it as my Get Out of Jail Free Card."

When there was no immediate response, Aguilar added, "If you'd rather have money, I can hack into the Anbessas' various accounts and get you whatever amount you want."

The disguised Solitaire just stared at the two bags.

"Do we have a deal?" Alberto asked hopefully.

There was no hesitation in her voice as the Secret Samaritan replied, "I'll take back what belongs to the Andrews and you can talk to the authorities about the rest," as she resealed the open bag.

"WHAT?" screamed Alberto, before releasing a long stream of unfavorable comments about women in general and the alleged Rosa specifically.

"Someone is bound to have called the Policía by now, if your mother hasn't over concern about our alleged relationship. Maybe you can work out something with them," said Solitaire, still speaking Spanish as she bent down to grab the drone box.

"Of all the…" Alberto began, before resuming his cursing. "If my damn bike had just started when…"

Solitaire simply smiled and walked away with the recovered stolen property, never mentioning having cut Alberto's rear most spark plug cable with the knife from her purse so the sabotage wasn't immediately noticeable before Rosa knocked on the Aguilar's front door.

CHAPTER 34

While her pace appeared nonchalant to any potential witnesses, Solitaire walked quickly to her van and entered through its rear door. A moment was all it took to secure the Andrews property in a storage compartment before Rosa sat in the front seat and drove away, passing a still tied up Alberto Aguilar before making a right turn at the next corner.

Even with the windows closed and the air conditioner on, she could hear a hint of sirens in the distance.

Solitaire drove at the normal speed limit and followed every traffic regulation while discretely doing what was needed along the way, like pushing the hidden button on the dashboard that caused the van to quickly display a different set of Florida license plates.

She was not surprised to soon see the flashing lights of a police car in her rear-view mirror.

Still within the residential neighborhood, Solitaire activated the van's right turn signal and parked in the first open space at the curb.

The police car stopped in the street beside her to block the van from pulling out again.

The driver rolled down the window and turned off the engine while waiting for the officers to cautiously approach, one on each side of the vehicle.

"Evening Officer. Can I help you?" the driver politely asked.

"License and registration," requested the uniformed man at the open window.

After receiving permission to reach into the front pocket of his coveralls for them, the man behind the wheel presented the items to the officer as Solitaire pretended not to notice his partner shining a flashlight through the tinted glass of the passenger window to get a better view of anything in plain sight.

"Art Cooke?" the officer asked the mustached driver, before reciting the local address off the license that was actually part of a Miami shopping center.

"Correct," confirmed the disguised Solitaire.

"The reason we pulled you over is because a crime was just committed in this neighborhood and we were wondering if you might have seen anything," explained the officer.

"Like what?" Art asked, while accepting the return of his personal identification. "The only person I've seen before you was someone standing beside a motorcycle."

"The suspect was driving a white van like yours," revealed the officer while briefly looking across the front of the vehicle at his partner.

"Really?" Art said in surprise.

Solitaire knew better than to turn in that direction and stayed focused on the man at the driver's window. But whatever silently passed between the officers must have been in her favor, because the flashlight beam disappeared.

"I didn't get a good look at the vehicle, but someone made a left turn at the intersection up ahead as I was coming on to this street," Art answered.

"Thank you for your cooperation. You have a good night now," the officer on the driver's side of the van said before racing back to join his partner at their squad car.

Within seconds the police drove past and turned left at the next corner as Solitaire started her vehicle.

Glad the quick change and everything else worked out, she happily thought before making a right turn at the same intersection moments later.

+++

The next morning Ariel Andrews was happy to receive the missing prototype and its data from Iris Higgins, but it was a new and improved XDS-2 that was eventually sold to the military and law enforcement agencies.

Despite prosecutors having new evidence of illegal weapons manufacturing and sales that introduced a wider range of Federal and International charges against him, César Fernandez pleaded Not Guilty to every accusation leveled against him. Yet before he could receive his day in court, the Anbessas' leader was killed in prison by members of the Royales gang that had been arrested when he used the stolen drone to expose their operation to the police.

Damián Garcia, César's amigo and right-hand man, vowed to avenge his Jefe but never discovered that it was the crooked police captain who had been with Juanita that covertly ratted out Fernandez to the angry gang.

Over time the rest of the Lions were tried and convicted for their crimes, but there was one suspect that Solitaire had to deal with personally.

+++

Carol Evans sat on her stool at the end of the cantina, content to slowly sip her drink and enjoy the solitude. A fútbol game was playing on the muted television mounted over the counter, but most of the customers were watching the event on the big screen set that occupied most of one wall further away.

It was a typical, peaceful evening in her new life.

Until he walked in.

The man was ruggedly handsome. A woman would have to be either totally blind or stupid not to give him a second look. Even from a distance, Evans could tell he had what some called smoldering eyes. The kind that could burn deep into your soul and expose everything a lady might want to remain hidden.

Coupled with his jet-black hair, at first she thought he was—but that was just an impossibility of someone Carol never wanted to see again.

He casually took a look around the cantina, then Evans' heart almost skipped a beat as the man came directly toward her. Despite the establishment's air conditioning, she felt hot as he stood next to her and asked in deep toned Spanish, "Is this seat taken?"

"No," she quickly replied with a smile as he occupied the neighboring stool. Then he motioned to the bar tender and asked for a cerveza.

Evans watched the man receive his order and pay more than the beer was actually worth, but never took so much as a sip as he just sat there and stared at her.

Finally, Evans couldn't help asking, "Aren't you going to drink that?"

"No," he answered. "One must keep a clear head around a beautiful Señorita."

Carol started to blush when the stranger added, "Besides, we have business to discuss."

"What business?" she wondered, growing concerned. There was a small handgun in the purse to her left on the counter, but could she get to it in time if necessary?

"About your future here in Ecuador, Carol Evans."

She almost choked on her liquor upon hearing her real name for the first time in months.

"César Fernandez died in prison," the man revealed.

"That name means nothing to me," she replied coldly, since he was at least partly to blame for her exile. Evans knew her boyfriend's hare-brain scheme of everyone signing over their rights and ownership wouldn't work, but he was too impatient and unwilling to wait the extra time required after stealing the drone to fully undermine Ariel and seize control of Andrews Aviation from within. While both were motivated by their own version of revenge, he wanted the company to provide a legitimate cover for his criminal activities while she planned to make it the foundation of her future business empire.

"Unfortunately, Reginald Andrews lost his battle with prostate cancer," the stranger added.

"On that, the Andrews family has my sympathy," replied Carol, not realizing she had just confirmed who she really was.

"He did dictate this letter to send his apologies," the man said, while pulling out a sealed, business size envelope from his lightweight jacket. "With the shock of receiving his cancer diagnosis and everything he went through since, Reginald honestly forgot to tell Ariel about his promise to promote you."

Evans stared at the envelope that now sat on the counter between them. "Too little, too late," she finally said, but pulled the letter over to lay by her purse. "Anything else?"

"Yes," the man replied, turning to look at her. "You're under arrest."

Carol Evans couldn't help but laugh at that statement.

The man just stared at her without comment until Evans finished. "You can't arrest me. Ecuador has no extradition treaty with the United States."

The stranger simply shrugged his shoulders. "Maybe not," he agreed. "Yet I never said I was arresting you," as he turned to look back at the cantina entrance. "Señor Gonzales of the Policia Nacional del Ecuador wants to have a candid conversation with you about the Anbessas, ghost guns and all the innocent people killed in his jurisdiction."

Evans spun on her stool and saw three uniformed men standing in the doorway. Upon realizing she was looking in their direction, the one in the middle gave her a big smile as he held out a pair of handcuffs for her to see.

The disguised Solitaire watched Carol Evans' face turn pale at the thought of being arrested in a foreign country, especially after having jumped bail and fleeing America before her trial.

"Well," Carol began, as she quickly turned away from the Policia, "if it's one thing I've learned from César, I'll find an official somewhere along the way that will let me go with the right bribe."

"Maybe," Solitaire agreed, maintaining the deep Spanish accent. "Too bad you're broke."

"What do you mean?" a confused Evans asked.

"Like I told the Policia before we tracked you down to this cantina, the fence you sold some of the Andrews Aviation stock to back in Mexico City gave you up after finding out those bearer bonds are fake."

"WHAT?" screamed Carol, loud enough to momentarily distract a couple of viewers from the game.

"I admit, it was a bit difficult tracking you from there to here," conceded Solitaire. "Changing your name and appearance was expected to some extent. But it was quite cunning on your part going from being a natural red head to dying your hair black to blend in better with the locals. Let alone either paying cash or… bartering for whatever you needed along the way."

Then Carol watched the stranger nod to the officers, which started the Policia moving toward them.

"Who are you?" Evans demanded to know, as the officer with the handcuffs drew near.

"Just a good Samaritan," Solitaire answered, maintaining the male voice of her disguise as she rose and left the cantina.

THE END

ABOUT OUR CREATORS

WRITER

LEE HOUSTON JR. - has been a writer and editor practically his entire adult life. After years of filler material for various community newspapers, he had been with the now shuttered Pro Se Press from the company's inception in 2010 as the writer-creator of *Hugh Monn, Private Detective* and *Alpha* the superhero, with several other short stories as well as working on past anthology magazines for the former publisher. While his complete bibliography can be found on his Amazon author's page, Lee's other creative credits include short stories for Airship 27, contributing to and co-editing the *Super Swingin' Hero 1968 Special* with Jim Beard from Mechanoid Press, editing the comic book mini-series *Raye Knight: Spellbound*, from Indy Planet, and serving as the Editor-In-Chief of The Free Choice E-zine (www. thefreechoice.info) since 2005. In what he laughing refers to as his "spare" time, Lee is an avid reader of pulps, science-fiction, detective/mystery stories, fantasy, and comic books. He maintains contact with readers via Facebook, e-mail via authorhoustonjrlee@gmail.com, Twitter, and his writer's blog at http://leehoustonjr.blogspot.com.

INTERIOR ILLUSTRATOR

CHUCK BORDELL - was born a poor transistor farmer in the rust belt of western Pennsylvania. His childhood was filled with polluted rivers that he fell in love with anyway, the sound of railroad cars crashing together, and dreams of lusty women of dubious reputation. Eventually, he tired of all things iron and decided to trade rust for heavy metals, moving to Missoula, MT in 1987.

Despite a decided lack of tree cover (comparatively speaking) he found Missoula to his liking and, after earning a degree in Archaeology in 1991, decided to stay and continue his quest for the world record two-headed trout. In the meantime, he discovered that he had some skill in telling stories through sequential art and has since worked for numerous comic book publishers, including Malibu Comics, Caliber Comics, Alpha Productions and Silverline Comics. He has produced artwork for Steve Jackson Games and Dungeon Magazine, along with various illustrations for the Neverworld RPG and the Superdeck Superhero Card Game.

His most recent graphic novel is called Lunatic Fringe and recent gaming books include GURPS: Traveller and Earthdawn: Dragons. The Ministry of Wolves, a military fantasy, has just been published by SynergEbooks.

COVER ARTIST

TED HAMMOND - is a Canadian artist who has been creating amazing art for over twenty years. His work has appeared in magazines, ads, books and graphic novels just to name a few. Go to (www.tedhammond.com) to contact him and check out more of his work!

ACKNOWLEDGMENTS

Due to several external matters, this was a hard novel to write. Suffering two different major computer crashes that each resulted in having to totally replace the system was bad enough. Losing a beloved family pet didn't help, but the passing of my father during the creation of this book was another matter.

My deep thanks go out to Nancy, Brian, Stacey, Zach, Terra Lynn, Jason, Ben, Frank, Wayne, Brenda, Teel and Roland for their support.